F

TUMBLING RANGE WOMAN

**Center Point
Large Print**

**This Large Print Book carries the
Seal of Approval of N.A.V.H.**

TUMBLING RANGE WOMAN

Steve Frazee

Center Point Publishing
Thorndike, Maine

This Center Point Large Print edition
is published in the year 2005 by arrangement with
Golden West Literary Agency.

The text of this Large Print edition is unabridged. In other
aspects, this book may vary from the original edition. Printed in
Thailand. Set in 16-point Times New Roman type.

ISBN 1-58547-530-0

Library of Congress Cataloging-in-Publication Data

Frazee, Steve, 1909-
    Tumbling Range woman / Steve Frazee.--Center Point large print ed.
        p. cm.
    ISBN 1-58547-530-0 (lib. bdg. : alk. paper)
        1. Large type books. I. Title.

PS3556.R358T86 2005
813'.54--dc22

                                                                2004014990

CHAPTER 1

South from the Columbine River they rode, across the long dry hills with the slow dust dripping into the sage behind them. There were two of them. A dun packhorse that had never known the feel of rope followed steadily, carrying camping gear and brand-new mining tools.

They had come from Mexico. This northern land of great blue mountains was strange to them in many ways and they looked upon it with differing views. Dallas McQuiston was pleased with the country. He was thirty, a long-waisted man who rode with the arrogant grace of a Comanche.

An Irish stubbornness and an Irish wildness in his features were gently tempered by the heritage of a Creole mother. Shards of humor sparkled in his long gray eyes. He rode a bay gelding with a spearpoint blaze and white stockings. There was a pistol on his hip and the scarred stock of a long gun slanted up from under his left saddle fender.

Beside McQuiston on a broad-rumped Mexican pony was Benevides Calistro, a somber man with the high cruelty of a petty hidalgo stamped on bold features. Discolored by time, silver inlays showed in the stock of his rifle. He carried his pistol in a Yaqui holster. In his expression he carried disapproval of all things seen in this new land.

At the meadows where Rough and Tumbling Creek crossed the Lake City road the two men stopped to let their horses drink.

5

"Is she worth the look—this woman?" Calistro asked.

"Who knows? They say two men have died because of her. Where we come from what better recommendation could a woman have?"

"One was her father." Calistro's dark eyes showed contempt of *gringo* ways, even the ways of McQuiston, whom he loved as a brother.

"Perhaps it was only talk that her father was killed because of her," McQuiston said. "It is easy to lie about a woman."

"You will look at her. You will smile at her and she will smile in return. All women do that for you. And then?"

McQuiston smiled at the far blue mountains and the reaching hills happy in the sun. "Why then we'll go on to the San Juan and find our fortune."

"I hear the words only." Calistro turned his pony up the Tumbling.

They passed a schoolhouse where two young men were sweeping. The youths stood on the steps and returned their salutes, eyeing the strangeness of their rigs and the packhorse that followed like a dog.

McQuiston said, "It's Sunday, Ben, I do believe. I'll bet they're going to have preaching there."

A few miles up the Tumbling they waited to let a wagon come around a sloping, rocky point. The driver was an ox-shouldered man with a red face so closely shaved the skin had a burned look. He stopped. His wife released her grip on the grab bar of the seat. She began to smooth her dress.

A woman riding near the creek to escape the dust now

6

turned uphill and came to the wagon. She was tall, with a skin as golden as the thin upland sun, graceful in spite of her position on a sidesaddle. Her black horse gleamed like wet satin.

"Headed for gold, eh?" the driver asked. His tongue rolled Scottish burrs.

"Aye," McQuiston said, and grinned. "How far would it be to the Three Bar Y?"

"The Darland place?" The man glanced sidewise at his wife. He had seemed disposed to pass the time of day and visit for a spell, but now he gave McQuiston and Calistro another shrewd going-over with his eyes and said curtly, "Two miles." He lifted the lines, rapping them up and down on the team, and started on again.

McQuiston turned to watch the girl on the black horse. She waited for a time after the wagon left, looking back at him curiously, and then she sent her horse downhill again to get away from the dust.

Calistro smiled and looked at the sky.

"I merely asked an honest question," McQuiston said. "Now I'm more curious than ever."

"There are women everywhere, and you are always curious. We will never get to the San Juan."

"Why hurry? I like the looks of this valley anyway. It could be a place to settle down, Ben."

"The woman on the black horse was like an Aztec princess," Calistro said. "She was—"

"It really is a fine-looking valley, Ben. It's possible— The girl on the black horse? She looked us over as hard as her father did. Her hair was faded in places from the sun. There was no mystery about her, except how she

7

could ride so well on a saddle like that."

"And she has not caused the death of two men."

McQuiston shrugged; it was his best defense against Calistro. Their friendship needed no questioning, but no *Yanqui,* not even one born in Calistro's village, could fully understand the man, for across Calistro's life there lay a long sigh.

It came, McQuiston knew, not from one experience or failure, but from many sources, from memories of creeping Indian terror in the time of the Mexican moon, from years of dealing violently in the strange and wonderful politics of Mexico—from many things—but most of all, from being born a true Mexican.

They rode on, with the packhorse walking free behind. They met another wagon, a second family going down to church at the schoolhouse, McQuiston thought. The man was tall, black-browed, with a strongly thrusting jaw. He pulled in his team and his eyes ran to the mining tools on the dun.

His wife was a small woman in faded black merino. McQuiston's thoughts lingered on her expression for a moment, and he wondered if the quietness had grown upon her in the winters of this northern land, when the wind was skirling snow across the sage flats and the Tumbling was running sullenly under blue ice.

He could have his flashes of Irish perception and quick Irish sadness, too. But he brightened when a gray-haired woman in the back seat said, "Howdy there, boys!" Her voice was deep, her manner like a hearty slap upon the shoulder. There were three young girls beside her and one upon her lap. She looked at the rigs of the two riders and spoke in Spanish, asking them where they were going.

Calistro bowed to the horn, sweeping off his hat. "To the San Juan, *señora*. We think we are miners."

McQuiston spoke in Spanish. "How far to the Darland place? We heard we could get a good meal there."

"Did you?" The old woman sized McQuiston up again. "Yes, you look like a man who would have heard. Haven't you got no grub on that packhorse?"

McQuiston grinned.

"It's a half mile," the old woman said, still speaking in Spanish. "I'm going back with you."

The driver said, "Are they asking about the Darland place, Ma?"

"Yes." The old woman was curt and defensive.

The man looked at his wife, their attitudes instantly reserved. The driver raised the lines to slap the horses. "Good luck with the prospecting, boys."

"Hold on there, Rodney!" his mother said. "I'm going back with them to visit June."

The woman beside the driver turned quickly. "But we're going to church. I think—"

"*I* think I'm going back," the old lady said.

"You started to church." The black-browed man seemed to be apologizing to his wife, rather than protesting to his mother.

"I've changed my mind," the old lady said. "There's folks around here that claim poor old Grandma Varnum is close to brimstone anyway, so I don't need to be reminded of it." She moved children and stood up in the wagon. "Move one of them horses in close here." She

9

shook her head when McQuiston dismounted. "Not that bay highbinder! The other one."

Calistro led his pony beside the wagon.

"Now, Ma—" Rodney protested, but his mother was already leaving the wagon. With one hand on the saddle horn and one on the wagon seat, she swung herself out and settled neatly into a sidesaddle position.

The pony quivered and started to sidle at the whish of skirts. "Whoa there, you brute!" Grandma Varnum said. She waved at her son. "Go on to church with the Copperwhaites and the Bissells and the rest. I'll go up to June's and keep Squanto Whitcomb and Avery Teague from murdering this young man." She looked at McQuiston. "Who are you two, anyway?"

McQuiston introduced himself and Calistro.

Rodney Varnum did not look at his wife when he said, "We'll pick you up after the services, Ma." He drove away. The girls in the back seat were bouncing up and down and yelling, "Good-bye, Grandma!"

"Mind you listen careful to the preacher!" the old woman yelled.

Calistro led his pony away. Grandma Varnum looked sternly at McQuiston.

"So, McQuiston! Like all the other young whelps who hit this country for the first time, you had to come up here to see what June Darland was like."

"No!" McQuiston said. "This happens to be on our way to the San Juan. Where'd you learn to speak Spanish?"

"Don't try to put me off. You came this way on purpose. Did you stop in Columbine?"

McQuiston grinned. "We're still dizzy from what we did there."

"I imagine," Grandma Varnum said dryly. "You heard the lies about June, and you were like any other curious man, so I'll put you straight. Her father took up Buffalo Meadows several years back. Her mother died one winter and old Fred was left with three girls. Men were already pestering around June, so Fred thought it best to move down here where the girls would be close to women.

"Young Max Roby was one of her beaus. You probably heard he made a deal with Fred, trading land down here for a marriage."

"I heard that," McQuiston said. "Did he?"

Grandma Varnum was bitter. "Yes, he did, but it didn't work. June wouldn't have nothing to do with the deal when she found out. Somebody got so mad about it that they killed Fred Darland soon afterwards on Squire's Hill when he was going back to the meadows for some furniture."

"I heard that too."

"Yeah," the old woman said. "Make up your mind now that nobody knows who did it."

"But somebody hung Max Roby for it."

"You got a general idea of the story," Grandma Varnum said. She gave McQuiston a long look. "How interested in this are you, anyway?"

"No more than natural, I guess. What happened to the sisters?"

"An aunt took them back east. June wouldn't go. She's got some range and some cattle, and two old riders who

11

worship her. She gets along."

"How come her father didn't prove up on Buffalo Meadows?"

Grandma Varnum said sharply, "How come you're asking?"

"Just a natural question."

The old woman had her doubts. "You may be a tough man, McQuiston, but don't let sudden ideas go to your head. You're handsome too, but I've seen a thousand like you, and some of them weren't worth shooting. The wisest thing you can do is eat your dinner at the Y and go right on after gold."

"Are you her guardian, Grandma Varnum?"

"I'll do, for want of a better. It happens I like June, too."

"Then you must be a little different from the general run of people I've seen so far on this creek."

"You saw my son and daughter-in-law. Emma wouldn't say hell if she was standing in it. Who else did you meet down the road?"

"A big red-faced man with his wife. A girl on a black horse."

"Angus Copperwhaite and part of his tribe. You paid particular attention to Evaleth, of course—the girl on the black horse?"

"I must have seen her," McQuiston said. "I wouldn't call her a girl exactly. You'd make a good sheriff, Grandma Varnum." He laughed.

"And you're already a woman chaser, Dallas McQuiston."

Calistro glanced toward the creek. McQuiston

12

observed that he was grinning.

"This Teague and Whitcomb y̶
they the two old riders at the Y?"

"No!" Grandma Varnum look
down. "They won't care for y
you that right now."

They approached a large ranchhous
logs on a bench near the mouth of a gulch
shoulders of the hills came out to break the valley
A burned slab sign hanging on chains from the hig
crossbar above an open gate said *Meals*.

"One other thing, since you've got a long nose for
details," Grandma Varnum said. "Max Roby's will left
this place and his cows to June. No doubt you've heard
lies about that too."

"Nobody said she hanged him."

"Don't joke about it, damn you, McQuiston!"

"I didn't mean to." The old woman's anger sobered
McQuiston. He looked at a saddled buckskin standing
near a corral, a powerful horse at least three hundred
pounds heavier than his own big bay. It was for a giant
who needed it, or else it belonged to a runt who wanted
to make himself feel bigger.

The man who came out on the porch a moment later
was big enough to be the owner of the horse. His hair
was a mass of reddish curls. His legs were like great
posts holding him rooted when he stopped. His arms
hung awkwardly. His stillness, his massive facial features, made him look like a large stone figure staring
from the porch.

"Squanto Whitcomb," Grandma Varnum murmured,

s all the introduction McQuiston ever had.
down to give the old woman a hand but Cal-
already at her stirrup.

dma Varnum dismounted spryly. "You've got a
ony there, Bennie."

alistro smiled. He watched Grandma Varnum go
ward the house. He studied Squanto Whitcomb, and
hen he glanced at McQuiston with an expression that
mixed a warning with disinterest.

McQuiston called to the man on the porch. "All right
if we unsaddle and slip the pack while we're eating?"

"Go ahead." Squanto's voice was slow and deep. He
watched the dun packhorse as it trotted belatedly into
the yard. After a time he walked stolidly across the yard
to where McQuiston and Calistro were unsaddling. With
his eyes on the mining tools, he said, "Slumgullion
Pass?"

"Do you mean are we headed there?" McQuiston said.

"That's what I asked, wasn't it?"

The even, grinding patience of the man impressed
McQuiston, but at the same time it irritated him.
Squanto's eyes were too small for his huge, smooth
face; they were cold blue, bedded under heavy, calm
brows. The man kept waiting for an answer.

"We might go toward Slumgullion," McQuiston said.

Squanto started to walk back to the house. McQuiston
let him go several steps, then said, "That is, if it suits us
to go there."

Squanto stopped and swung around. He looked
McQuiston over thoroughly, and then, as if discovering
nothing he had not seen the first time, Squanto went on

to the house. The porch thumped under his weight.

McQuiston looked at Calistro, who showed a blankness that said he was not concerned with anything that might happen.

An old man came from a bunkhouse on the side of the hill, walking with the crabbed, pinched-in gait of one who has spent his lifetime in the saddle. Grayness underlay his weathered brown face.

Squanto called from the porch, "Clinton, June wants you to ride up on Spring Creek to ask—"

"I'll ask her myself what she wants me to do." Clinton went on to the corral, merely glancing at the two visitors. He saddled a long-legged sorrel, and it was a Texas rig he put on, from the broad horn to the cinching.

McQuiston asked, "How long since you been home?"

"A long time." Clinton hesitated. For a moment it seemed that geography held in common would start him talking freely. He studied McQuiston and Calistro, as if the sight of them brought sharp remembrance of years that had flowed over the horizon; and then all at once he withdrew his interest and became a sour old man again.

He rode to the porch, dismounted and went inside. He came out shortly afterward and went up the road. McQuiston saw how he held himself, trying not to show the stiffness time had hooked into him.

McQuiston and Calistro met June Darland.

CHAPTER 2

McQuiston's first impressions were of fragile purity, of girlishness hovering close to the line of womanhood.

15

She was a slim woman of medium height. Her hair was black, gleaming like a freshly broken block of tar. Her eyes were orange-brown, like the eyes of French women McQuiston had seen in Mexico.

The impact of female, full and tantalizing, came from her like a delicate odor; but still McQuiston could not find the easy words that had always served him at such times. He smiled mechanically, but mostly, he was staring.

June Darland looked back at him so intently, reading things about him, reaching her conclusions, that McQuiston was sure she was no up-country ranch woman with simple curiosity. And he saw, too, that his impression of fragility was wrong. The woman's arms were gently rounded, her throat full and strong.

She dropped her gaze under McQuiston's forthright stare. Her complexion was very light, but even against the darkness of her hair, with its suggestion of bluish undertones, her skin was not pale.

She raised her eyes suddenly and gave McQuiston an amused, probing look. Her lips tended toward thinness, but when the corners of her mouth lifted, as they did now, her mouth took on a full aspect.

McQuiston thought it was no wonder they stirred foulness about her. She was beautiful. It was a failing of men to slur beauty and the nature of women to tighten their eyes and pick to pieces loveliness in their own sex.

McQuiston flashed a glance at Grandma Varnum. She was standing in the doorway of the kitchen, watching him like a fierce old hawk. *I've seen a thousand like you, Dallas McQuiston.*

In honest admiration McQuiston bowed before June Darland. He tried to be reserved, to show her only a pleasant face and casual interest. "My friend, Ben Calistro," he said.

Calistro's courtesy lacked nothing that he had given Grandma Varnum; but there was a difference that McQuiston sensed immediately, mockery, smooth pretense. McQuiston thought June Darland saw it too, but she said, "I'm glad to know you, Mr. Calistro." She smiled. "You're Spanish, aren't you?"

"I am a Mexican," Calistro said, with pride.

Grandma Varnum said, "Someday I'll explain the difference to you, June. Let's eat."

Squanto had been silent, sitting at the far end of the room beside a cold fireplace, the bulk of him bulging a chair that creaked to his every small movement. He did not join the others at the table. His attitude did not seem to bother the women, McQuiston observed.

Grandma Varnum glanced at Squanto now and then, but June paid him no attention at all, as if he were an old and useless member of the family, waiting out his time in a chimney corner. McQuiston could not accept the big man so easily; his heavy presence kept pricking at the outer edges of McQuiston's consciousness, although he was watching June most of the time.

She was a woman to stir a man unreasonably. One glance at her had been enough to assure McQuiston that the evil spoken of her was baseless gossip. He said, "Do you have dances, as well as church, in the schoolhouse down the road?"

"Sometimes," June said. "More often we have a dance

17

here—some of us." She gave McQuiston a direct look.

"When's the next one?" he asked.

"Saturday night."

Squanto moved noisily in his chair, his scarred boots rasping against the stones of the fireplace. McQuiston gave him a swift glance, and then he looked at Grandma Varnum. The old woman was watching him narrowly, warning him.

June ignored McQuiston for a time. She put her interest on Calistro, smiling, asking him questions about Mexico. Calistro was polite, but once more McQuiston knew his manner covered a fine contempt for June Darland. And June, with a perception that startled McQuiston, seemed to be aware of the fact.

A horse came into the yard and Grandma Varnum said, "Here's Teague. He's ahead of Billy for once, and you're ahead of both of them today, Squanto. How come?"

"I ride slow," Squanto said, "but I start early and I know where I'm going."

June went to the door. The man who came back with her was of medium height, sparely built. He wore a trimly fitted black coat that fell away from the dark butt grips of a pistol. His hair was blond and silky and he smoothed it with his hand as he stood with his hat at his side, looking around the room with quick intensity.

"Well, Squanto," he said, "I see you stole a march."

"I take my time, Avery. I get where I'm going."

June introduced Teague to McQuiston and Calistro. The man waved carelessly. His lips were a curtain that whisked away from small, even teeth to make a semblance of pleasantness. To McQuiston Teague looked like a restless man, a man with slashing ambition.

"Don't let me interrupt your meal." Teague hung his pistol belt on a rack and went over to sit beside Squanto. They talked of a rider who had gone on a shooting spree in Columbine. They talked as easily as if they were alone.

But after a time they were quiet, and McQuiston saw their glances on him and knew they were waiting for him and Calistro to finish the meal and leave.

Two silent men did not bother June Darland any more than one. She did not glance at them. If they were suitors—McQuiston thought it likely—they seemed to be wasting time. There was at least one more, this Billy whom Grandma Varnum had mentioned.

McQuiston watched June Darland and took his time with the meal, and he noticed how his deliberateness was irritating Teague. A half hour passed.

June stood beside McQuiston at the rack near the door, holding his hat while he buckled on his pistol belt.

"You're just passing through the country on your way to prospect, Mr. McQuiston?" June asked.

"In a way, yes."

The attention of the woman made an area of pleasantness. McQuiston took things as they came, aware of but ignoring the listening silence, the air of hostility in other parts of the room.

"Have you ever ranched, Mr. McQuiston?" June asked.

"Ben and me have done that too. In fact, we've talked some of looking around this country for a place to light."

McQuiston did not look at Calistro.

"That would be nice."

"Let the man go, June," Squanto said. "He's on his way to do some prospecting. Let him go."

June did not give Squanto the satisfaction of a glance. She smiled at McQuiston. "Pay no attention to Uncle Squanto."

Avery Teague laughed. "Now that's what she thinks of you, Squanto!" He slapped his hand down on Squanto's leg, and Squanto knocked it away with a vicious, explosive move of his forearm.

McQuiston was watching the two of them. In one snapping moment when the smile winked off Teague's face as Squanto knocked his hand away, McQuiston saw a sharp hatred between the two. It was like a deep, warning growl in Squanto; it was a hot, flashing wickedness in Avery Teague.

Not once did June look toward them. She said to McQuiston, "If you should stay around the country until Saturday, come here for the dance."

"Thank you."

Calistro put money on the table. It was an insult, the way he flipped it carelessly, with the high cruelty of his face starkly clear. He looked at Squanto and Teague. He recovered his hat and pistol from the rack. After a bow to Grandma Varnum and June, he went outside, but he did not leave the porch.

McQuiston lingered deliberately. Grandma Varnum came over and said heartily, "Find a lot of gold, boy!" Her eyes were hard as she made a small nod toward the door with her head.

McQuiston's last impression of the room was June Darland watching him with a half smile, and from their chairs at the fireplace, Squanto and Teague staring.

Calistro went down the steps with McQuiston. "I've seen you sneer like that when you were laughing at some *puta* in a cantina," McQuiston said. "What's the matter with you, Ben?"

"In a cantina one expects—" Calistro turned to watch a man on a rocketing steel-dust. The rider came around the shoulder of the hill suddenly, and his horse was beautiful with surging power as it galloped down the road. At the gate it turned like a cutting horse and picked up its speed at once. Its sudden stop was more spectacular than the run.

The rider came down in a careless leap. All haste was gone. He dropped the reins and sauntered toward the house, a young and handsome man, rangy, dressed in striped pants and a dark gray coat. His movements spoke of youthful recklessness.

McQuiston made his swift observation and went on to the corral. He stopped near the saddles and looked back. The rider who had just arrived met Teague coming out of the house and said, "Hello, Avery. You're early. What—"

"Hello, Van Buskirk." Teague returned the greeting curtly, in such a preoccupied manner that Van Buskirk swung around to watch as Teague crossed the yard.

McQuiston heard June Darland say, "Come in, Billy." Van Buskirk saluted her and then he walked down the steps and followed Teague.

"Trouble," McQuiston murmured to Calistro.

Calistro shrugged, as if to say, *What can one expect when he rides with you to see a woman?* He stooped and took a rawhide rope from his saddle and made a pretense of observing something wrong with the pack.

Teague came up smiling. "To make things very clear to you, McQuiston—Miss Darland was merely being polite when she asked you to come to the dance here."

"I thought it was very polite of her," McQuiston said.

Teague's bare pretense of friendliness vanished. "Don't come. Understand?"

Van Buskirk came up. "So that was it? I'll say it too, mister, don't come."

McQuiston gave Van Buskirk a quick look. There were youngsters like him everywhere, leaping toward trouble without a thought, as recklessly as this one had ridden into the yard.

Teague said, "This is my affair, Billy."

"It belongs to three of us," Van Buskirk answered.

Several steps away on McQuiston's left, Calistro said, "Two on this side." Thereby he took responsibility for Van Buskirk away from McQuiston.

"What kind of trouble are you looking for, Teague?" McQuiston asked.

The flare of wildness behind Teague's eyes was like the sudden gushing of flames from a smoldering fire. In an instant McQuiston knew him: A tightly strung man who could rise to killing anger quickly, a man whose mind was always leaping and twisting, even when his face was quiet.

"I'll take anything you have to offer," Teague said. "Right now is the time, McQuiston."

The deliberate prod at McQuiston's combative instincts was hard to overlook. Delivered anywhere else, it would have been met as it was given, but this was June Darland's yard. From the edge of his vision McQuiston saw her on the porch. There was rough talk about her in plenty already. A killing here on her doorstep would ruin her reputation.

McQuiston turned away from Teague. "Let's go, Ben."

For most men, that should have been enough; it gave the field to Teague.

But it was not enough for him. "McQuiston! You didn't say that you understood."

McQuiston turned back. Out of pride and out of temper and from the cold knowledge that so far he had always been a little better than any man who had forced him to test his pistol skill, he almost took the step that Teague wanted. But he heard June Darland say, "Can't you stop them, Squanto!" and Squanto growled a reply that was not clear.

"I understand what you said." McQuiston stepped toward his saddle again.

And still it was not the subjection that Teague wanted. He narrowed the proposition down to where there could be no turning away without defeat. "Get clear out of the country, McQuiston. Understand?"

McQuiston came around for the last time, ready to meet the challenge.

Van Buskirk made a quick move. Calistro's rope flicked out, a flat cast that dropped around Van Buskirk's neck. The reata did not touch his shoulders before Calistro snapped it tight and jerked him off his feet. Van Buskirk broke the fall with one hand, the other digging to get between the rawhide and his neck.

The tension between McQuiston and Teague hung like the shadow of a knife.

A rifle blasted and a bullet ripped a corral pole. "I'll kill you both, so help me!" Grandma Varnum shouted. "You're a pack of snarling curs!" The action of the rifle clashed as she came across the yard.

Teague and McQuiston stared at each other. Van Buskirk rolled, reaching for his pistol, clutching the thin line around his throat with the other hand. Calistro jerked the rope again. He stepped forward and kicked Van Buskirk's elbow. The man cried out in pain and fury.

"Tromp the young fool into the ground!" Grandma Varnum yelled. She came up behind Teague. "You'd kill right on her doorstep, would you! So will I then, if one of you makes a move!"

Their pride held Teague and McQuiston still locked in a silent duel.

"Take that rope off him, Calistro," Grandma Varnum ordered.

That gave McQuiston and Teague the chance to look away from each other. They watched Calistro roll slack into the reata with a turn of his wrist. He put his hand on his pistol. Van Buskirk loosened the rope and hurled it away. With one knee still on the ground he started to draw his pistol.

Calistro's pistol was clear when Grandma Varnum shot in front of Van Buskirk. The bullet broke the hard packed earth in little chunks and grains of soil slashed into Van Buskirk's face. "You crazy old fool!" he yelled. He took his hand away from his pistol and rose.

Grandma Varnum cut loose her fury then. McQuiston knew how scared she had been, because now her fright turned into unholy anger that lashed four silent men.

"Get out, the bunch of you! You're no better than prowling dogs! Get out!" The old woman spun around and waved her rifle at Squanto. "And you too, Squanto Whitcomb!"

"Yes," June said quietly. "All of you go." She watched them for a moment and then she turned and went slowly into the house.

Calistro put his pistol away. He picked up his saddle and went into the corral. Van Buskirk started to follow, and Teague said viciously, "You've bollixed things enough already, Billy. Nobody asked your help."

"You didn't do so well." Van Buskirk fingered his throat.

Once more McQuiston saw hatred standing between two of June Darland's suitors. They were indeed like snarling curs. He kept an eye on Teague as he picked up his saddle.

Squanto came rocking off the porch. He got his buckskin and swung up. In the saddle he was still a lumpish, awkward-appearing man. He stared at Teague and Van Buskirk and nodded toward the gate. The three rode away together.

Three men who hated each other. McQuiston looked at Calistro but the Mexican was in no mood to comment on the strange ways of *gringo* suitors.

25

Grandma Varnum said, "I told you not to hang around here, McQuiston. I warned you. Now beat it, and good luck somewhere else." Her hands were trembling on the rifle. She marched back to the house.

The riders were out of sight and Calistro was making a last check of the pack ropes on the dun when June walked over to McQuiston.

"I'm sorry, Miss Darland. I didn't want—"

"It's all right. Teague is always quarrelsome. I suppose I shouldn't have asked you to come back." The woman smiled wistfully. Great sympathy for her rose at once in McQuiston.

"You had the right to ask me," he said. "Who comes to your dances?"

"Mary Bissell, once. Sometimes Evaleth Copperwhaite when she can sneak away from her father. Grandma Varnum." The smile died. "Mostly it's just Squanto and the other two."

The striking purity of the woman's expression was shadowed with a loneliness and a yearning that struck deep into McQuiston's sympathy. He thought of the three men who were besetting her and a look of wildness came to his face. He said, "I'll come here Saturday, if you really want me to."

June gave him a steady look. "It might make trouble. It's up to you." She shook her head. "I suppose it's best if you don't come back."

"Am I still invited?"

"Yes, but . . ." June lowered her eyes. There was an air of abiding sadness in her manner that aroused McQuiston against the attitude of the country, and made

26

him brutally angry against the three men who had gone up the road. They were making misery of this woman's life!

"You say you've ranched?" June asked.

McQuiston nodded.

"There's some wonderful meadows not far from here, almost a thousand acres. It belongs to no one, so far." June described the place and the way to it, pointing. Her face lightened with pleasure as she talked.

"It's odd," McQuiston said, "open land like that in this country." He glanced at Calistro.

"It's there," June said, "with all the range around it that anyone can hold." Doubt edged her tone. Her eyes went over McQuiston, studying him slowly, and then suddenly she turned away. She said good-bye in a voice that indicated he had not deserved her interest in the first place. McQuiston watched her as she walked toward the house. A curtain moved. Grandma Varnum was seeing all she could. The door closed behind June and McQuiston kept staring at the dark boards. The dun moved restlessly.

"Shall we go now?" Calistro asked.

"You don't like her, do you?"

"I did not say it."

CHAPTER 3

They rode away. McQuiston looked back, puzzled because he could not clearly recall all details of June's appearance. "What are you holding against her, Ben?"

Calistro was looking at the horse tracks in the road.

"The three are the ones who hanged a man who was to marry the woman."

"They're a pack of wolves! They act like they owned her."

"Perhaps they are the protectors of the woman."

"Why do you call her 'the woman'?" McQuiston said. "You know her name."

"Is she not a woman?"

"Say why you don't like her, damn it! Just because she's a *gringa*, is that your reason?"

"The old one's a *gringa* too. I like her. That which I did not like, my friend, was a strangeness, a fear in the air about the place, like the touch of dead fingers, like sitting in a lonely *jacal*, while knowing that the *coraje* was creeping down on me."

Coraje. The madness that comes of boredom, of loneliness and vastness in the hot lands of the South. It had nothing to do with anything at the Y; but Calistro was a man of deep moods, with the mysterious mixture of yearning and understanding that is purely Mexican, and so he often said strange things.

It was much more pleasant to think about June Darland.

After a long time, Calistro said, "The great-barreled horse of the one called Squanto had been broken gently."

"I didn't notice." But Calistro would have noticed, for he was a man who loved horses and who could bring them to the saddle with great patience, or break them quickly and savagely, depending on the animal.

They rode on beside the bright river until they came to

28

a place where a narrow meadow broke into the steep drop of the hills on their left. McQuiston stopped. "This is the way she said to go to Buffalo Meadows."

"Yes," Calistro said, his tone affirming only the fact McQuiston had stated.

McQuiston grinned. "There may be a great mine up there. Who knows? But if not, haven't you always wanted a castle high in the hills, with fat cows grazing as far as your poor eyes could see?"

"Once I wished to be ruler of Mexico." Calistro followed when McQuiston left the road, trailing old marks of wagon wheels along the toe of the hill. "I was a general then. Now I go with a man who rides where a woman says he is afraid to ride."

"She didn't say that, Ben."

"Is there another reason we go this way?"

"I heard some talk of these meadows in Columbine. If they're what people say, what's wrong with taking them up? We'll never settle down looking for gold. I wouldn't mind having a ranch."

"You believe what you say?" Calistro asked.

"Yes!" McQuiston thought about it then, and strangely enough, he did believe his own words. Although Calistro did not know it, McQuiston had gone a little farther in Columbine than merely listening to idle talk of Buffalo Meadows. Still, his decision seemed to need bolstering. "It's not just that a pretty woman mentioned the place, Ben. If Grandma Varnum had said—"

"If the old *señora* had spoken of the place, I would be riding fast to get there."

"I know," McQuiston said. "I saw how well you

thought of her. She likes June Darland. Why is it then that you—"

"I have said nothing of the young woman who is beautiful to you."

"You sure get the job done left-handed." McQuiston shook his head in exasperation, and then he laughed.

The way led upward on an easy grade. The meadow sharpened and dwindled to nothing against a great ridge on their right. The road turned left into a bowl hemmed by sage hills. Ahead were pale green aspen ridges and then crests of dark timber against a faultless sky.

"It's up there beyond the pines, Ben, a wonderful country."

"In winter it is cold."

"She said it wasn't bad."

"It is not cold in winter," Calistro said.

McQuiston sighed. "You've been damned hard to get along with ever since we made the turn on the Tumbling. Shall we turn back and go prospecting?"

"Yes."

"I knew you'd say that."

"And I knew you would not hear."

They rested their horses part way up a steep hill. Squire's Hill, for there was a mound of brown rocks here, a slab that said *Fred Darland,* and against the willows of a small creek below was the graying wreckage of a light wagon.

McQuiston looked all around. He guessed the bullet bad come from the timber off to the right; somebody waiting with a rifle. But that was of the past. On ahead was Buffalo Meadows. His interest in

30

the grave died and he went on.

Calistro lagged, turning to look back.

A half hour afterward, when they were following the trace through tall aspens on another hill, Calistro said, "There is something not good about these Buffalo Meadows, yes?"

"Something odd, of course, but not necessarily bad. We'll find out in time."

"That is surely true." Calistro made a thin smile.

They rode with the scent of the pines around them, emerging from the trees on a grassy plateau, and that led them onward until they came at last to Buffalo Meadows.

The sight struck McQuiston hard. Here was a richness that only a man from a dry, hot land could appreciate fully. There was no wind. A thousand acres of grass stood motionless, pale green in the sun. A foot high on the edges of the gently sloping basin, the grass ran down to tall lushness along the bottom of the park, where a shining stream made slow loops.

All around the meadows, following the outline of the dark timber, was a high log fence, zig-zagging its way on widespread legs.

Nowhere in all the greenness stood a cow, and there were no cows in sight on the range outside the fence.

"Beautiful!" Calistro murmured, his face sharp with wonder. "Why is it so that no one owns this?"

"All I know is what she said." *Nobody owns it, so far.*

Far away, near the lower end of the park, there were a cabin and a corral, forlornly gray against the richness of the meadows. Those marks of human labor, and the tremendous fence of darkening logs, gave McQuiston his moment of uneasy thought.

Buffalo Meadows was a prize to make men kill each other. Fred Darland had taken it up. He must have been a workhorse of a man to build the tremendous fence, but now he was gone, his family scattered, only June still living in the country.

And it did not appear that anyone had been near the place since the Darlands moved.

They rode down to the cabin, slowly, looking at the meadow as they went. The structure was set on dry, level ground, just above the beginning of the seep that fed the tall grasses. The door was closed, the windows shining blankly in the afternoon sun. McQuiston felt an odd hesitancy about disturbing the silence, or intruding in the cabin.

He rode off to the left, where he saw stonework standing above the grass. He looked down into the square of a waterbox, deep and cold and clear. The bay kept dipping its head. McQuiston rode on down into the overflow and let the horse drink.

He looked across the meadows. In spite of the fence and the cabin, the park gave back an impression that it had been untouched, and that the fence could not enslave it.

When McQuiston returned to the cabin, Calistro pointed toward the hill behind it. A rough headstone with pine needles sifted in a pile around its base sat at the end of a mound in the triangle formed by three tall trees.

"The mother?" Calistro said.

"I suppose. Grandma Varnum said June's mother died here several years ago. Can't you see anything besides graves today?"

A calmness overlay the cruelty of Calistro's face as he mused. "In the winter, perhaps, it was, when the loneliness was running with the cold, and there was a great silence on the meadows." He nodded. "Yes, he was right to take his children from this place."

McQuiston, whose heart was Mexican, but whose head was as hard as any Yankee's, understood Calistro's feelings, but he could not share them. "You see too far for me," he said.

"I can see my own grave here, if we stay." Calistro smiled. "But there is a grave waiting somewhere for everyone, and this is a beautiful place."

They went inside the cabin.

It was a big room, which made its bareness all the more of a shock. In one end was a fireplace, and there was a tin-covered opening for a stove pipe in the roof, but there were no furnishings of any kind. The walls were tightly fitted, the hewed flooring closely set. No rats had got inside; the room gave the impression that no living creature of any kind had been here for a long time.

Once there had been wooden pegs in auger holes in many places on the walls. Someone had broken them all off, leaving the bright serrations of the shattered pegs flush with the logs.

They went outside and closed the door. Calistro got on his pony and went through the corral, out into the meadow. He rode leisurely, going up the park, then back and forth across it. Near the stream in the middle the grass was belly-high on his mount.

McQuiston went over to where the woodpile had been. Someone had burned whatever was left of it after the Darlands left. High bunch grass made a ring around the place. He saw two fire-reddened hinges that might have been on a cupboard, the charred handle of a broom, part of one of the pegs that had been broken from the walls.

He picked up the corner of a slate still set in the angle of the frame. It might have been June's. He tossed it down and went to the corral to wait for Calistro.

The Mexican returned unhurriedly. He said, "There is no bog. I thought perhaps there was and that the fence had been built to keep cattle out, instead of in. The grass is good. There never have been many cows upon it."

"That bears up what I heard in Columbine."

"There was more than hearing," Calistro said.

McQuiston nodded. "I looked into it at the court-house, just briefly."

"I have been thinking so. I am glad that it is not all because a woman said to come here. Who gives the land?"

"We can stake a hundred and sixty acres. The rest we hold the best way we can. I love the place already, Ben."

Calistro watched McQuiston's expression as he looked at the park. The land was not home to Calistro; it was not Mexico or even the great Southwest which was almost like Mexico. Yet it was good for McQuiston, for *Yanquis* were not fitted to live forever under the long suns of the South, not even the best of them, which were very few.

"I am for staying," Calistro said.

"I'll go to town tomorrow to make the filing."

"And you will return by the way of the Y, about the time of the dance?"

"I might."

"I will be here, but not in the house." Calistro pointed. "Somewhere in the trees."

"What's the matter with the cabin?"

"There is no place to hang a bridle."

McQuiston began to unlash the pack on the dun. "We'll stay in the cabin tonight, at least."

CHAPTER 4

Squanto Whitcomb, Avery Teague and Billy Van Buskirk left the Y together in a cloud of frustrated anger, ready to snap and bite at each other at the least pretext.

Squanto gave more than a pretext when he said, "How's your neck, Billy?"

Van Buskirk had been feeling the rope burn on his throat. He jerked his hand away. He cursed. "I was in the middle of it. Remember that. You stayed on the porch."

"The odds were even." Squanto was calm. "There wasn't any call for it, and you both made damned fools out of yourselves."

The flashing wickedness in Teague came up in his stare. For an instant he balanced between lashing out at Van Buskirk, who had horned into a quarrel, and answering Squanto, who had done nothing. Teague chose Squanto. "It would have pleased you, wouldn't it, if McQuiston had shot me?"

Squanto seemed to chew the question for a moment. He said, "Yeah. If he'd got either one of you. That would have been one less man getting in my way around June. Does that answer you, Avery?"

Teague was stunned momentarily. "By God, yes!"

Squanto was a picture of calm good humor. It was hard to tell about him; it always was. His answers on any critical matter were so blunt that Teague always kept sniffing for trickery and evasion.

Right now Squanto was grinning. It occurred to Teague that the expression might be from the sheer joy of being in a scrap, verbal or otherwise; but Teague could not accept the idea. It was simpler to assume that Squanto had something up his sleeve.

"Not that you two are going to be anything more than nuisances in the long run, anyway," Squanto said. "I'll outlast you both."

"What do you mean by that?" Teague asked quickly.

"I mean I'll still be there after she's sick and tired of your meanness, Avery, and of Billy's half-baked showoff stuff."

"Showoff, huh?" Van Buskirk said. "I ran you off my range on Cathedral Creek. I—"

"You did that," Squanto said.

Teague and Van Buskirk glanced at each other. For an instant they were allies, but it did not last, for Teague's viciousness was too close to the surface. "You horned into my fight, Billy. You'll do that once too often."

"You couldn't handle both of them!" Van Buskirk's temper narrowed. "I'm not sure you can handle McQuiston alone."

"You want to go any farther with that?" Teague stopped his horse.

Van Buskirk reined in. His eyes were hot and steady. "I'll go as far as you want, Teague."

He would, too, and Teague knew it. Young and wild and violent, Van Buskirk had all the grit he needed and some to spare. Squanto turned his horse and sat apart, watching them quietly.

Three men who had once been friends, still bound by the habit of friendship—and other considerations. They knew each other's strength and each other's weakness, and they could quarrel heatedly, insulting each other, with no great damage done.

But now two of them had pushed beyond the point where they could fling an easy insult and turn away. They had sharpened a moment to a glittering point, and there time hung.

Squanto said, "Go ahead, kill each other, boys. Remember what I said about one or two less?" He saw the temper run from the hard edge that lay between Teague and Van Buskirk. They stared at Squanto, giving him their rage. He was unarmed. He was careless. He turned away from them with a laugh.

"You'll go too far with that, Squanto," Teague said. "You run around without a pistol. You insult—"

"Listen to me!" Squanto had been a colonel of infantry during the Civil War, and now his voice roared as if once again he were trying to reach a whole regiment. "She's had a hell of a life since we—since Max Roby was hung. Every time I go to town I hear whispers around me and it's all I can do to keep from cracking heads in every saloon in Columbine.

"How do you think June feels? She won't be able to live in the country if we shoot each other up or hurt any man who goes near her. Is that what you two want? Are you trying to drive her away, you idiots?"

Squanto spoke with terrible patience, with logic that eased the rage between Van Buskirk and Teague.

Silent then, the three men resumed their ride. After a time Squanto said, "Aside from what it would do to June, I don't want to see you two shoot each other."

"The hell you wouldn't!" Teague said.

"I'll marry June, no matter what you two do."

Squanto's arrogance was no shock to Van Buskirk. Secretly, Van Buskirk had always admired the quality and had tried in his own way at times to imitate Squanto. But old Squanto was wrong this time. Van Buskirk was the youngest of the three, the best looking. He knew it, and his confidence was hard to shake. He said, "We've already got a bet, Squanto, or I'd lay some money with you that you're not going to marry June."

Avery Teague made no joke of Squanto's bluntness. No man was forthright unless he was trying to obscure some trickery. Van Buskirk was a wild young fool who didn't know enough to keep out of another man's fight. He would ruin himself with June. But Squanto was dangerous, for he tried to hide cleverness under a cloak of frankness.

"If you're so concerned with what a shooting would do to June's reputation, why didn't you try to stop me and McQuiston a while ago?" Teague asked.

"I figured to, but Grandma Varnum was ahead of me."

Squanto grinned. "I'd say she handled it all right."

Van Buskirk's face changed. He felt his neck, jerking his hand away when he thought the others might notice. "Where were those two going?" he asked.

"Over Slumgullion." Squanto looked hard at Van Buskirk. "You asked for what you got, Billy. Don't think about making it any worse, because it will fall back on the Y. All the two of you had to do was keep your mouths shut, and those fellows would have been on their way by now."

"She invited McQuiston to come to the dance," Teague said. "Did you see the way he looked at her?"

"I saw," Squanto said. "But you lost your head, Avery. You're always too ready to jump any outsider that looks at June. If McQuiston comes back, it'll be because you told him not to." Squanto shook his head. "But he won't stick around. He's got too much common sense."

They came to the gate of Teague's place. Like all the ranches on the Tumbling, the buildings here were only a few years old, but unlike most, they had a permanent look. Teague was a fussy man about appearance. He was also a reserved man when it came to having visitors, and so it was with grudging courtesy that he said, "The cook will have something hot on the stove, if you care to come in."

Squanto shook his head and rode on. Van Buskirk stopped, turning his horse to look down the road.

"Maybe Squanto's right," Teague said. "Let's not worry about them."

"You didn't have a rope around *your* neck," Van Buskirk said. "The next time I'll be ready for that move."

39

"Yeah. What'd you do to start it, anyway?"

"I was trying to bluff the Mexican," Van Buskirk said. "I made a pass at my pistol, but I didn't mean—"

Teague cursed wildly. "You tried to bluff! You idiot! I was betting my life and you tried to bluff! You're lucky Calistro didn't use a pistol instead of a rope."

"I'll know better the next time," Van Buskirk said. He stared down the road. "They ought to be in sight. We rode slow. Do you suppose they're still at June's?"

Teague did not answer. For a time he had been sure that his man was scared, and then, when McQuiston had turned that last time, the wildness of him had been a shock. Still, that was no proof of the man's courage, or his pistol skill. It rankled, this unsettled affair; but secretly Teague wondered if he had not been lucky. Allowance of that was doubly rankling.

Van Buskirk said, "They should be along by now. Where are they?"

"They had a horse to pack," Teague said. "They'll be by. And when they come, just let them pass." He studied Van Buskirk shrewdly. "Haven't we got enough trouble with Squanto already—me and you?"

Van Buskirk refused to step into the opening. He gave Teague a quick look, and then he turned once more to look down the road.

"You going to eat with me or not?" Teague asked.

"I'll stay awhile." Van Buskirk spun his steel-dust and followed Teague into the yard. "Do you suppose they knew about Buffalo Meadows?"

Teague had started to dismount. He settled back into the saddle. "They're prospectors."

"Everybody who rides through the country hears about the meadows, Teague. That's where those last two, the brothers, got their big idea—just from loose talk."

"You'll think up any reason to jump that Mexican, won't you?" Teague swung down.

"Why ain't they in sight?"

"Maybe they camped. They might have done anything. They'll be along, Billy."

"They wouldn't camp between here and the Y, not if they were really headed for Slumgullion. They're still at June's or else, by God, they've gone up toward the meadows!"

"That's too damned much at once," Teague said. "First, McQuiston makes a play for June and she acts like a fool, and then you decide he knows about the meadows."

"How could they ride.through the country without knowing?"

"Sure, maybe they did hear. A lot of people have. How many have tried anything?" Teague stared down the road. He had started to take his horse inside a corral, but now he dropped the reins and left the animal in the yard.

They waited an hour. It was Teague's patience that began to splinter first. He had eaten while Van Buskirk watched, and then the two men sat at the kitchen table, with their attention on the road. Teague kept drinking coffee. When it was gone, he threw the pot in the woodbox and cursed Joe Emory, the cook.

"All right," he said, "just to satisfy you, let's ride back and see what happened to them."

Van Buskirk grinned.

On the way down the road Teague said, "We ought to settle things about the meadows, Billy. That crazy agreement we made—"

"It suits me. Squanto hasn't made any objection to it, either."

"You and Squanto wouldn't be trying to rig up something between you, would you?"

Van Buskirk's eyes narrowed. "I'm all for myself in that deal, Teague, and you know damn' well that Squanto is too."

Once more Teague showed his native distrust of a straight-forward declaration.

They rode to the meadow where Darland's scratchy road began. "What did I tell you!" Van Buskirk jabbed his finger toward the tracks. "Prospectors, you said!"

"Maybe they are, after all. But if they ain't, how the hell was I to know different?"

Van Buskirk started up the meadow on the trot.

"Wait a minute, Billy!"

Van Buskirk wheeled around, his horse rearing. "What for?"

"This is Squanto's business too, you know."

"Are you afraid without him?"

"I warned you about saying—"

"All right, all right." Van Buskirk swung his horse to face up the meadow again. "What do we need Squanto for? Besides, this trouble won't have anything to do with June."

"He ought to be in it. It's his risk as much as ours. It seems that you and me have been doing a lot of

Squanto's work lately, Billy. He sits back—"

"I'm going up there," Van Buskirk took off on the trot again.

Teague hesitated. He kept seeing the picture of McQuiston and June talking near the door at the Y, ignoring everyone around them. "Slow down!" he called.

He rode to join Van Buskirk.

At the foot of Squire's Hill Van Buskirk observed how unerringly the riders had gone on, with no casting around to find the dim road. "They knew where they were headed."

Teague stared upward, frowning. They passed Darland's grave. Van Buskirk gave it a quick look, but Teague did not even glance toward it. Before they crossed a gulch that was a rough boundary between rocks and aspens, Teague stopped his horse suddenly and said, "This is far enough, Billy. I'm not going up there today."

Van Buskirk wheeled around impatiently. "Why not?"

"Squanto is home, just hoping something like this will happen. Why was he so sure they were going on out of the country? He wasn't. No, Billy. I'm not going out to get killed while Squanto sits home and laughs. Tomorrow we'll all come up here together."

Teague turned and rode down the hill.

His sudden defection left Van Buskirk grinding with anger, but not enraged enough to defy all reason. He took one last look up a narrow lane in the aspens, and then he followed Teague. They went back to the road in silence.

When they reached Teague's gate, Van Buskirk said, "I'll tell Squanto tonight. We'll be here in the morning."

Teague nodded. He went on into his yard.

A man of strange, bitter moods, Van Buskirk thought. Teague was given to sulking, or falling into spells of depression, and then he would come flashing out of the depths in a crazy, dangerous way.

CHAPTER 5

Grandma Varnum was weary. Running a pack of quarrelling men from the yard had sapped her emotional energy. For an hour, after helping June with the dishes, she read the Bible, her lips moving as the words passed slowly into her mind, a long forefinger dropping down the pages line by line.

She rose once and went into the kitchen, where June was bathing in a copper tub. The old woman studied the slender form critically. "You'll do, Junie, although I will say you could stand a little more flesh on you."

June smiled. "I worry it off."

The old woman nodded. "I know." She went back to her Bible, sitting in a straight chair at the table. There was a rocker in the room, hauled down from the abandoned home at Buffalo Meadows. Grandma Varnum remembered how June's mother, tired at thirty, had used the rocker during the last few years of her life.

At seventy-two, Grandma Varnum was tired herself, but a rocking chair was a mark of old age, and she would not be seen in one. She let the Bible close gently at last, looking down at her hands.

They were old hands now, toughened by work, scarred in the long struggle, but their character was not ruined. Jim Varnum had remarked upon their beauty long ago, which had been an unusual thing for a man to do, for the men whom Grandma Varnum—then Carrie Moffatt— had known in early womanhood had scarcely paused to see beauty of any kind.

Jim Varnum. Half dozing at the table, the old woman saw him clearly, a brown, tough Texan with blue eyes and a slow smile. They had been married in New Orleans. Two months later, Jim Varnum had returned to Texas to settle an estate, and he had been killed in a senseless quarrel with two cousins.

Not even the bare details of his death came to her until a few months before Rodney was born. Her life had been hard enough before her marriage; it was much worse after Jim's death. With the tall barrier of the years thrust aside, Grandma Varnum looked back and felt no shame, and saw no way she could have changed things. She had done the best she could.

She dozed, remembering Jim Varnum and the brief time they had been together.

June said, "How do you like this dress?"

Grandma Varnum raised her head with a start, unable to break instantly the tenuous strings of the past. She saw June, the freshly scrubbed beauty of her, the form of her turning lightly in a simple, gray-flowered dress, and she saw the graceful play of June's hands in the air.

No, I was never like her, never beautiful; but I was young and he loved me. I deserved the love he never lived to give. What happened afterward could not be helped.

"I don't know how you have the time to sew," Grandma Varnum said. "It's pretty, June."

Suddenly motionless, June said in a small voice, "Do you think there'll be a time when any of the older women will stop here?"

"I'm about as old as they come. I stop here."

"You know what I mean, Grandma." The vitality was gone from June. "The things that have happened—were they my fault? I never had anything to do with Max Roby, except to be nice to him."

"That was all, huh?"

"If you don't believe me, then I haven't one friend. I—" June ran across the room and knelt, weeping, with her head in Grandma Varnum's lap. "The way they go by here, pretending to look straight ahead . . ."

The old woman stroked the glistening hair, feeling rage against a situation that could not be helped at once. "Cry it out, June, cry it out."

After a time June rose, drying her eyes on the hem of her dress. "You believe me—what I said about Roby?"

Grandma Varnum nodded, staring out the window.

"What can I do to change things?"

"Get married," the old woman said bluntly.

"I don't want any of those three."

"You keep them coming here."

"I can't keep them away as long as they behave."

Grandma Varnum sighed. "Billy Van Buskirk has the makings of a man. He's hard working, in spite of his crazy ways. He's young and good looking. Don't you like him?"

"I like him, yes, but he's just a wild young kid."

"Well, you'll have to settle on one of them, or you'll have to send them all away. The women are *not* going to let you live here alone forever. Believe me, they won't. They'll make it so miserable for you—"

"They have already! That's one reason I refuse to tell Squanto and the others not to come back, even when I don't want to see them." June went to the window. "Here comes a wagon now."

"I see it. That's Rodney. I'll have to go on home now."

June went across the room swiftly. She put her hand on Grandma Varnum's shoulder. "Couldn't you stay? Couldn't you stay here and live with me?"

"I never thought of it." It would quiet the gossip, sure enough. Grandma Varnum stirred the idea slowly.

"It's none of my business," June said, "but you don't get along with Emma. If you—"

"Emma's all right, considering she's a daughter-in-law. A little pious, maybe, but she's all right, in her way."

"It wasn't fair to say anything about her. It wasn't fair to ask you to come here either." June straightened her shoulders. "It's just that I'm so lonely all the time."

"Maybe you ought to sell the place and move to town."

"I've thought of it. Angus Copperwhaite is the only one around with any cash. He made an offer once to buy the place, but you know Angus."

"Tighter than a bull's—Yeah," Grandma Varnum said. "You want to stay here, is that it?"

"Of course! I grew up in this country. I'd be lost any-where else."

"Then stay. We'll work it out somehow."

"If it wasn't for you, Grandma Varnum, I couldn't face it. I couldn't stand it when—"

"I haven't been much help, June."

The wagon approached the gate. They saw Rodney Varnum speak to his wife. She shook her head. Rodney stopped in the road. He leaped over the wheel and stood a moment as if ashamed of the discourtesy he was about to do, and then he strode into the yard.

"Nine tenths of all the hell in this world is caused by piousness," Grandma Varnum said. Rodney was tall and strong like his father, but a woman had told him it would taint his children if he drove them into the yard, and he had obeyed. In fairness, Grandma Varnum allowed that Emma was gentle and reasonable and never holier-than-thou, except about June Darland.

With a smile June opened the door. Rodney had a shamed look, a guilty flush under his dark skin. He removed his hat and held it awkwardly in big hands.

I wonder if he's ashamed of me too, Grandma Varnum thought.

"Howdy, June." Rodney fingered the brim of his hat. "We're ready to go home, Ma."

"Won't you come in?" June held the door for Rodney. She glanced past him, at the wagon.

"I just—" Rodney saw where she was looking. "Yes. Thank you." He stepped inside.

Grandma Varnum stared at him harshly. "What did the preacher talk about, Rod?"

"I don't remember, off-hand. Why?"

Grandma Varnum raised her Bible like a shield before her chest. "From the way you've acted since you stopped that wagon, I don't think anyone spoke from—"

"Don't, Grandma," June said quickly. "Let's not—"

"—from the same Book I've been reading." The old woman shook her head. "I won't go home tonight, Rod. I think I'll stay here with June until next Sunday. You and Emma come by then, and if she'll let you drive into the yard long enough to pick me up, and if you're not afraid that it'll cost you your immortal soul, maybe I'll go to church with you."

Rodney considered the words. His eyes were steady. "All right." He made a small bow to June and went out.

"You can't force people into thinking this is not an evil place," June said. "I don't want you quarrelling with your family over me."

"There was no fight. Rod understands."

"But his wife never will, and neither will any of the other married women of this country."

Tired, with all the anger suddenly gone from her, Grandma Varnum watched her son go back to the wagon. His walk, too, was like Jim Varnum's. But he was not Jim. No, he was Jim's son, and he was all right, and Grandma Varnum loved him no less than she had his father.

It had been a long time since Grandma Varnum had given over to the unrewarding pastime of looking into the past. Suddenly she knew what had started the trend this day: That young McQuiston whelp. She had not realized it immediately, but his whole manner had reminded her of Jim, his natural grace, his slow smile, and the way he held amusement behind a grave expression.

June said, "Why didn't you like Dallas McQuiston?"

The old woman gave her a startled look. "I liked him well enough. It was just that the last thing you need around here is another man making trouble. I told him that."

"Do you think he'll come back?"

Grandma Varnum studied June shrewdly. She saw a curious mixture of youth and innocence housed behind a calm, mature manner. The girl probably did not realize how much trouble she could cause between men; but it was time she came around to knowing the fact.

The country of the Rough and Tumbling was not a cantina or a dancehall, where a pretty, clever woman, for the sheer devilment of it, could play men against each other until they killed in the excitement of their lust. Grandma Varnum had a dark moment of doubt; but she knew she was wrong. June Darland was not like that.

She was merely in rebellion against unfair, harsh censure, and she was fighting back with the only power she had.

"Do you think he'll come back?" June asked.

"McQuiston? To the dance? To be mangled by Squanto and those other two plug-uglies?" The old woman shook her head. "He'd be a fool."

"I suppose he would." June turned away. A tiny smile moved her lips.

"What did you tell him when you went out to the

corral after the trouble?" Grandma Varnum asked sharply.

"I told him I'd made a mistake. I told him he'd better not come back."

"That was sensible."

CHAPTER 6

Shortly after dawn McQuiston and Calistro were up and packed. They left nothing in the cabin but the ashes of their fire. McQuiston watched the light growing on the meadows. "How many head could you hold there all winter?"

"Enough," Calistro answered. "But that will be later, and it will depend upon the winter."

"You're still going to hide out in the timber until I come back?"

"Yes. I'm becoming a great coward."

McQuiston rode away, heading toward Columbine in a straight run across the hills. The sunrise came pouring in on his right and he greeted it with a Mexican song. When he sighted gallows frames on a hill, he swung toward them and came into the mining camp of Broken Forge.

He looked with distaste on the yellow dumps spreading in the sage, on the piles of clean timber that would be sent down to rot in the earth, on the clutter of buildings in a narrow gulch. He stopped long enough to water the bay. From here there was a road to follow.

In early afternoon he was at the land office in Columbine, a small room on the first floor of the domed courthouse. George Lawson, the clerk, was a portly man with a bartender's haircut, steel-rimmed glasses, and gray beard stubble that he rasped gently with the edges of documents while he talked.

"So you're back again, eh, McQuiston? Did you have any trouble finding the place?"

"No. Now I want to file on it, four forties smack up the creek."

Lawson rubbed his chin with a paper. "You weren't so enthusiastic before."

"It was only idle curiosity before. I might not have even looked at the meadows, but something changed my mind."

"Oh?" When Lawson realized that he was going to get no enlargement of McQuiston's statement, he asked, "Have you got the ground staked?"

"Yep," McQuiston said blandly. "The same corners as the original filing."

"I imagine," Lawson said drily. Sheets humped and slid smoothly in the big book he opened. His glasses came down on his nose as he peered at the numbers of townships and sections. "Here it is. You'll be the fifth one that's filed."

"Why didn't Darland prove up?"

Lawson shook his head. He lifted one corner of a page and scratched his chin. "I don't know."

"What about the others?"

Lawson shook his head again. He lifted a pad and placed it on the book and began to copy figures. "It'll take you five years, you understand."

They finished their business. Lawson leaned on the

counter, rasping his whiskers with the papers. "You look young and healthy. Maybe you'll last it out."

"I think I will." McQuiston started out.

"All I hear about that land is rumors. If you care to ask in the sheriff's office, Charlie Nye may have the straight of it. He's the deputy."

The man just settling down to write in the jailer's book in the sheriff's office was slim, with thin, pleasant features, mild brown eyes, and receding sandy hair. He glanced at McQuiston, nodded, and dipped his pen.

Beyond the desk, glaring out from a cell, was a brutish looking man with disheveled hair and blood on the side of his face. The man at the desk asked, "What's your real first name, Utah?"

The prisoner said, "You find out."

McQuiston watched the pen move on the white sheet. *Utah Smith . . . Murder . . . possessions on person: two pistols* . . . The man blotted the writing carefully. He closed the record and looked inquiringly at McQuiston.

"I'm looking for Charlie Nye."

"That's me."

He did not fit McQuiston's idea of a lawman; a desk deputy, no doubt, jailer and general handyman. "I just filed on four forties up the middle of Buffalo Meadows."

Nye looked at McQuiston's pistol, at his general bearing; he sized McQuiston up slowly and carefully, and then waited for him to go on.

"What kind of trouble can I expect now?"

"Are you alone up there?" Nye asked.

"I've got a partner."

"Yeah, I remember. You and the Mexican. You two

pried up hell around here a few nights ago."

"We had a time," McQuiston admitted.

"Who sent you up to Buffalo Meadows?"

"Nobody. I heard about the place here in town, so we went up and had a look at it. Now I've filed on it. What makes you think somebody sent me there?"

Nye's manner in ignoring the question was so vague it left no offense. He said, "A man named Darland was on that place long enough to get the patent. Why he didn't, I never understood."

"He was killed."

"Yeah."

"Why?" McQuiston asked.

Nye shook his head, watching McQuiston steadily. "After that, a tough Missourian named Len Corbett made a claim there. His horse came in one day on the creek above Squanto Whitcomb's place, but we never did find out what happened to Corbett.

"There were two others then that didn't stay long. Then the Shepherd brothers showed up. They were hard enough for anybody. They had a run-in over the place with some people up that way. One of them was wounded and both of them was dragged clean across the hummocks of the meadow behind horses. They were still spitting blood when they came in here to sign a complaint."

"Against who?"

"Three men. Avery Teague, Squanto Whitcomb and Billy Van Buskirk."

"So?" McQuiston asked.

"At the last minute they decided against signing the

complaint. I was the only one here, and after looking me over, they said they didn't think nothing would come of a warrant nohow. They left town." Nye smiled faintly.

McQuiston said, "For all the running-off that's been done, there still isn't a cow on all that grass."

"There never was, after Darland took his stuff down on the river."

"I'm going to hold the land, Nye."

"It ain't the world's best. It's pretty high to winter cows, unless you want to stack and feed. There's better places in the San Juan, I hear."

"I like Buffalo Meadows," McQuiston said. "What you're saying is, I can't expect help from the law if I'm jumped, is that it?"

Nye was slow and stubborn and undisturbed. "No," he said, "that ain't it. Within the limits of the law, you'll get the protection any man is entitled to. But if you need help real bad, you know as well as I do that it'll be too late for anyone down here to give it. You asked what you were getting into. I've told you."

"I see. Darland is shot off his wagon on a hill. The man suspected of doing it is hanged by somebody. Another man disappears and is never found. Yes, I see where the limits of the law are."

Nye was still undisturbed. "Max Roby was found four days after he was hung. During three of those days it had rained. Not even an Apache could have made anything of the sign that was left."

McQuiston nodded. "I didn't come in to quarrel. I know how big the country is out that way." He glanced

55

idly at the sullen man gripping the cell bars. "Who brought him in?"

"I did. Why?"

"I just wondered." Nye would do, even if he did not look the part.

"Nobody sent you to Buffalo Meadows, huh?"

McQuiston shook his head. The deputy's stubborn insistence was irritating because McQuiston knew that he himself was lying a little about June Darland's part in the venture. But after all, she hadn't sent him to the meadows; she had influenced him some, that was all.

He rode down the main street of Columbine. The yeast of boom was here, end-of-the-rails, supply center for a mining rush, and the very heart of a tremendous ranching country. In McGruder's Mercantile he bought a two months supply of food, a water bucket and a few odds and ends to supplement the scanty cooking gear of a pack outfit.

At the Bartley Mining Supply Co. he bought a cook-stove still in its heavy oak crate, and at a lumber yard he ordered boards and nails and light tools to make furniture. He found a bearded teamster who said he could haul all the purchases to the meadows within a week. The man didn't know where the place was so McQuiston started to draw a map.

"Never mind," the teamster said. "I'll ask my way, and I cain't read no map nohow."

"I don't want you asking your way."

The teamster grunted. "Like that, huh?" He doubled his price, and McQuiston told him to go to hell.

Mining companies were paying freighters high rates.

It was three days before McQuiston found another teamster willing to take his job. The man said it might be the middle of the next week before he could make the haul. McQuiston paid him ten dollars in advance.

Afterward, standing at the Tomichi House bar, with all his town business settled, McQuiston worried briefly about Ben Calistro. But Ben would be all right; he was like a shadow in the hills.

The sight of well dressed gamblers reminded McQuiston of something he had overlooked. He went out and bought a dark broadcloth coat and a pair of black and gray striped pants. His boots looked shabby then, so he took on a new pair. He was ready now for the dance at the Y.

This was Thursday. There was no reason why he should not return to the meadows, but he decided to wait another day and go directly to the Y. If he went back to the cabin first, Calistro would insist on accompanying him to the Darland place to back him up in case of trouble. Van Buskirk might be there, and he would never forget what Calistro had done to him.

Of course, there was the possibility that June would not allow any of the three suitors to return Saturday. McQuiston smiled at his rationalizing. He knew what he was: A man headed straight into a foolish act.

He was in Mark Finlay's dance palace when a handsome, painted woman shoved in beside him at the crowded bar. "You look lonely, mister."

"That could be. Shall we have the drink first, or the dance?"

The woman's smile was frank. "With you, the dance

might be enough, but I do have to make a living." She kept studying his face while they were out in the jostle of the dance floor. "When they get a far-away look like that, it's either a big mining deal or a woman. Which is it with you, mister?"

"You're making wild guesses, beautiful." McQuiston grinned.

The music stopped and she said, "It's a woman. You might as well have been dancing with Shorty, the bald headed bartender over there." Her expression was a mixture of wistfulness and failure and anger.

When McQuiston went to get his horse on Saturday, the liveryman was leading it out when suddenly he began to curse and sidestep as kittens poured out of an empty stall. "Git, you varmints!" the liveryman yelled. "Scat!"

The empty stall sucked the kittens back in again and the man came forward, shaking his head. "You got any mice at your place?"

McQuiston considered a moment. "Plenty," he said. He went into the stall and picked out one of the kittens, a broadfaced tan one with a tail that stood like a wedge. "Is this a male?"

"Hell, how would I—Sure!" the liveryman said, and both he and McQuiston laughed. "Better take two. Company for each other."

"I don't think we got that many mice." McQuiston put the kitten into his coat pocket. It climbed out promptly and started up his side.

"If you're riding far," the liveryman said, "you'd better let me give you a sack."

"I'm going up the Tumbling, but I think this tiger will ride without a sack."

"Beautiful country, the Tumbling. I know Squanto Whitcomb up that way. I once seen him wrap his legs around a pony, grab a big limb overhead, and lift the pony off the ground. Great fellow, Squanto, a little hard to get to know, but once you're acquainted—"

"I've seen him," McQuiston said. He rode away.

The kitten was all over him for a while, climbing, mewing. Once it got behind the saddle, and when its claws touched the bay's rump, McQuiston had some fast action before he got the horse quieted. But at last the kitten went to sleep, its head and paws sticking above the top of the coat pocket.

It was a cute little bugger; June would love it. McQuiston hummed an old *vaquero* song as he went toward the Y to keep an appointment with a lady.

CHAPTER 7

In the middle of a bright morning, Billy Van Buskirk rode ahead of his two companions until they came to the grassy drainage break a mile from Buffalo Meadows. Squanto, as usual, had been in no hurry. Van Buskirk had been forced to wait while the big man ate breakfast, shaved, and spent an hour giving advice to an itinerant horse-breaker.

"We still got the tracks," Van Buskirk said. "They knew exactly where they were going."

"Hold up," Teague said. "Let's swing into the timber here and come in on the cabin that way."

Squanto grunted his disdain of such tactics. He went on down the middle of the dim road. His lips a little thinner, Teague caught up and rode beside Van Buskirk.

When they came in sight of the meadows, they stopped. No horse was out on the grass, the corral was empty, and no smoke came from the cabin.

"This is a good way to get killed," Teague said, "riding straight in on a place that looks deserted."

"Got a guilty conscience, Teague?" Squanto's stare brought the temper to Teague's face, but Squanto grinned at him suddenly. "Remember the day we all showed up here when Mrs. Darland was washing, and she ran us off?"

"I remember." Van Buskirk kept watching the cabin. "I liked June's mother—and old Fred too."

A silence not entirely from the tension of their watchfulness fell upon them as they approached the cabin. Van Buskirk hailed the place. His voice ran out across the meadows and was lost.

Van Buskirk swung down and went inside. He came out a few moments later. "They stayed here. There's new ashes in the fireplace."

Teague said, "We should have burned the place down when we cleaned everything that was left out of it."

"No harm done." Squanto, squinted at the meadows. "They stayed overnight and cleared out."

"How do we know they cleared out?" Teague asked.

"All right." Squanto shrugged. "Let's look around and see which way they went."

That took an hour of slow work. Darland's claim

stakes were still in the meadow, rotting, fallen over, dark with the snows that had soaked them. Teague found where three horses had gone north, after taking down and replacing logs in the fence.

"Headed for town!" Van Buskirk cried. "They went in to file."

Squanto chewed his lip. "And took the packhorse? Looks to me more like they might have headed for Broken Forge to stake a mining claim."

"We don't know that," Teague said.

"Nope." Squanto looked at the timber and yawned. "But I ain't about to follow their tracks all day just to find out where they went. All we're interested in is if they're here."

"I've got a notion to follow their trail," Van Buskirk said, "just to be sure where they headed."

"If that's all you got to do, go ahead," Squanto said. "I got horses to break and a fool trying to do the work for me. You're sore because you tried your luck against Calistro and got the worst of it. Teague here is biting himself because he still don't know whether he could've beat McQuiston or not in a pistol fight."

Squanto started back across the meadow. Shortly afterward the other two caught up with him.

"The bet still stands?" Teague asked.

Squanto was slow in answering. "Yes."

The day they dragged the Shepherd brothers across the hummocks they had made the wager. Buffalo Meadows was to go to the man who married June Darland. Squanto knew how the bet had tickled the raw wildness of spirit in Teague and Van Buskirk; but to

61

Squanto the wager had been most practical for two reasons.

It had helped to settle an uneasiness among the three of them. True, they had worked together in running off anyone who tried to hold the park, but the arrangement had been that of three wolves who knew they would fight later over the common spoils. The second reason was quite simple: Squanto was going to marry June, and she wanted the park.

Squanto recognized the enormous arrogance inherent in the affair. He suspected that the other two had never given that aspect of the arrangement a second thought, for this was a land well named—Rough and Tumbling—where weakness was failure.

"We're going to stick to the agreement, the losers don't make any trouble?" Teague asked.

"That'll be up to you two," Squanto said, "since I won't be one of the losers."

Teague smiled. He was the only pistolman of the three. If he lacked other qualities, he did not allow the thought to trouble him.

Van Buskirk grinned and said, "I'll let you two bastards stand up with me at the wedding. As far as I'm concerned, you two lost the bet when you made it."

He took his horse in a surging jump across the creek. He went on to send it over a low place in the fence on the south side of the meadows. The other two got down to take out rails when they reached the place where he had crossed.

All three of them raced toward the break that led down to the Tumbling.

On the ride toward the sage they almost reached a relationship they had once known. Their talk was easy, full of jokes. Van Buskirk sang a song he had heard in Rose Watkins' place in Columbine two weeks before. They might have been young hellions who were the best of friends, with no property or ambitions—or strange bets—to throw a shadow on their carefree spirits.

But when they passed the grave on Squire's Hill, the small furrows of uneasy quietness came upon their faces. They were silent as the horses crunched along the rocky hill. When the hoofs were making softer sounds in the wash beside the willows, Squanto said, "That Corbett fellow up there—what do you suppose happened to him?"

"Up there?" Teague asked. "What do you mean?"

"I mean the fellow whose horse drifted in on the Tumbling last fall. My God, man!"

Squanto's flash of impatience caused Teague and Van Buskirk to look sidewise at each other. They gave Squanto no answer.

Bound strongly by distrust, they went on toward the Tumbling without further talk. Billy Van Buskirk thought morosely of the days when their friendship had been a bright quality, when they had jostled with each other for land and range, fighting, savage at times, but learning respect for each other in the conflict.

Now there was a cloud upon their relationship; he wondered if it would leave when their pact was broken by marriage of one of them to June Darland. Van Buskirk liked the salty give-and-take of tough-minded men in friendship. It was a shame, when they had recaptured for a time the old way of being, that the sight of something like Darland's grave could cleave coldly between them.

He knew what had happened: Seeing Fred Darland's grave had reminded them of Max Roby, and there was where the shadow had fallen on them—the day they hanged Roby.

But how could they have known he was innocent? From the very start everything pointed to Roby's guilt. His very nature indicated it. He was a hot-tempered man with a Southerner's contempt for those who did their own work. He had never had to fight for land on the Tumbling, but had bought everything he wanted.

And then he had tried to buy June.

When he discovered too late that Fred Darland could not make his daughter carry out the bargain, what was more natural than that Roby should be in a killing rage against the father.

Both Squanto and Van Buskirk were on the range when they heard of the Darland killing. It was two days before they got together with Teague, and then the three of them went to see June. Van Buskirk remembered it well. June was still shocked and she cried when they talked to her and she was ashamed when she at last told them of the agreement her father had made with Roby.

She told them the whole story. She had not known of the marriage arrangement until the day before her father's death. Roby had come to the Y that day and she had told him she would have nothing to do with him.

"He acted like a wild man," June said. "He claimed he

had made a will in my favor and he told me about the land he had deeded to my father. He said he could tear up the will easily enough, but he said the whole country would laugh at him when they knew how my father had tricked him. He even accused me of being in on the trick."

That was the Roby they knew, a man with pride that could not stand laughter.

"What did he say when he left?" Squanto asked.

"He said nobody was going to make a fool of him," June answered.

Van Buskirk asked, "Did he know your father was going to the meadows the next day?"

June pressed her hand against her forehead. "I don't know." She looked up in time to see the expressions they gave each other. "No! Don't do anything. I don't think Max would have—"

They were riding away. They went to Roby's house, and there the cook said Roby had gone to Old Agency the day before Darland was killed, and was not back yet. With a sullen sky above them and a rage smoking in their hearts, they started toward Old Agency.

On Los Pinos Pass they saw Roby coming toward them. His guilt was evident, for he stopped his horse and watched them for a few moments, and then he turned and ran for it. They chased him through the timber when he tried to lose them. They shot his horse from under him and piled him up in a tangle of fallen trees. They accused him.

He stood bare-headed with his arms across his chest to ease the pain of a broken shoulder. "You goddamned savages!" he said. "Just because she's going to marry me—"

"No use to try to throw us off," Teague said. "We know you killed Darland."

"I didn't know he was dead until this morning!"

"Why'd you run from us?" Squanto asked.

"I would have been a fool not to, knowing you three. You've found out that June is going to marry me, and so—You're savages! By God, you're worse than savages!"

Rain was beginning to fall. Everything that Roby said rang like a lie in the gloomy forest. They tied his arms behind him and put a loop around his neck. Then they flung the rope over a branch of the nearest tree and put him on Squanto's horse.

"Go over to Old Agency!" Roby cried. "Ask the Dudley's when I got there. It was the day before Darland was killed."

"How do you know when he was killed?" Teague asked.

"You said he was on his way to Buffalo Meadows! If he went there the day he said he was going to, it was the day after I last saw June."

Everything screamed guilt, but Roby did not look guilty to Van Buskirk, and now that the deed was in the making, reason made a strong appeal. With a dry mouth Van Buskirk said, "Maybe we ought to—"

His words were lost in a pistol shot that scared Squanto's horse into a lunge that dropped Roby into the air, jackknifing his legs, swinging.

With a horror like a snake in his belly Van Buskirk

watched Roby die. His whole being shocked into rebellion against the savagery of it, Van Buskirk finished a sentence that was too late, ". . . go see if he's telling the truth." But he never knew whether he said it aloud, or whether it was merely a protest that muttered through his mind.

Even today he did not know who had fired the shot.

They rode away from Roby. Teague said, "He was guilty as hell." The other two echoed the statement and hurried away under the cold spilling of the sky.

Later they knew the truth, from the Dudleys and from a seven-man land survey crew that had been staying at Old Agency: Roby had come there the day before Darland was killed, and he had stayed there until the day he was hanged.

Van Buskirk was not a moody man. He defended himself fiercely. *How could we have known he was not lying?*

Yes, it was the hanging that had brought the strangeness among them, darkly, quickly, like a hideous plant rising overnight from a rotting log. The sight of Darland's grave this day was too much remembrance.

Van Buskirk tried to forget everything.

He found himself lagging behind, when ordinarily he would have been out in front, kicking his dust in the faces of the others. Squanto's great buckskin was a hundred feet ahead of Teague. Van Buskirk adjusted himself to the present: The hanging had been a mistake, but it was done; thinking about it was no good. But still a detail snagged in his mind.

He caught up with Teague. "Avery, who scared

Squanto's horse with the shot that day?"

Teague watched Van Buskirk for an instant, and then he made a little nod, looking ahead at Squanto. Teague asked a question of his own. "You started to mumble something that day, just before the shot. You were still talking afterward, but I never caught the words."

"I said maybe we should have checked up on his story about being at Old Agency."

Teague nodded, his eyes intent. "I was thinking that when the horse jumped."

They both looked at Squanto. Van Buskirk felt better. They had managed to transfer a large part of their guilt where it properly belonged. Soon afterward Van Buskirk was able to push the whole incident into some dark recess of his brain. There were other things more immediately important.

He said, "I'm still not satisfied that those two left the meadows for good. I'll scout around up there one of these days before long and make damned good and sure."

"Don't get excited about anything you see until Squanto is with us."

They could distrust Squanto and combine to shift blame upon him, but they must have him with them when the going was rough. Sly politics. Their whole relationship was like that now. Van Buskirk did not like it, but that was the way they were joined. He had another moment of gloom, remembering the days before rage overpowered their judgment on the Los Pinos.

Van Buskirk had as much work to do as any man who owned a place on the Tumbling. He did not neglect it.

On Saturday he went alone to Buffalo Meadows.

From the timber at the upper end of the park he scanned the empty meadows. There was no sign of life at the cabin. He had brought a lunch with him, thinking to wait most of the day; but patience without an objective clearly in sight was not part of his character. After a restless half hour he went around the park through the trees until he cut the tracks that he had seen earlier in the week.

The marks were old now, mushed into the sandy ground under the pines. He followed them. After a mile his face leaped with an expression of sharp satisfaction. Two of the horses had turned off to the east. Van Buskirk took up the trail, with the swift elation of the hunter instinct spurring him on.

He didn't need Squanto and Teague. He'd show them how careless they had been in assuming that Calistro and McQuiston had left the area. The trail led across the open hills toward Rock Creek. It ran out suddenly on the great slabs of stone above the stream. Van Buskirk stopped at once. He had his own pre-conceived ideas about this exciting game.

He went straight to the nearest spit of timber that angled back toward Buffalo Meadows. He was wrong; his man had not gone that way. He made three more bad guesses before he settled down to a slow, systematic search.

At last he made the strike. His quarry had doubled back and he had overrun the tracks in his haste. Even then it took another hour to unscramble the trail. Van Buskirk entered the timber and stopped. A smile bunched one side of his face. The fellow with the pack-horse was headed back to Buffalo Meadows.

No doubt he was camped somewhere close to the park in the timber, waiting for his partner to return. Van Buskirk was wary now, and he could base patience on the possibility of running into an ambush. He rode with his rifle in one hand, having a great deal more faith in his ability with a long gun than with a six-shooter.

When he knew he was getting close to the lower end of the meadows, he left his horse and went on foot, and that increased the zest of his stalk. Any thicker than usual clump of timber might deliver up the enemy, or any drop into a gulch where trickles of water ran.

He found the camp. No tracks led directly to it, but a horse whickered softly and revealed the location.

Van Buskirk dropped to the ground. He could hear the horse stamping around. He began to ease in, and after a short crawl he saw the dun packhorse watching him from a rough corral of ropes and dead trees around a small swamp.

He kept edging in and at last he was satisfied that the horse was the only living thing in the camp. Soon afterward he discovered fresh tracks leading west. He kept prowling around. The fresh tracks were the only evidence that anyone had ridden away from here since the camp was made.

On top of a small rise beyond the corral Van Buskirk could see down into the lower end of the meadows. One man had gone into town; the other had stayed here to watch, and he had probably been in the edge of the timber laughing to himself when he saw how easily Van

Buskirk and the other two had given up the other day.

The thought angered Van Buskirk. Still, he was pleased with his accomplishment. He considered for an instant that he had been lucky to find the camp when the man was gone, for otherwise the dun would have caused trouble. But luck was part of his life.

He went down to where the trees thinned out near the toe of the ridge, peering out at the meadows. He was about to turn away when he saw the rider come out of the timber at the upper end of the park and head to the right, down toward the Tumbling.

It was not McQuiston; Van Buskirk would have known the bay. This was a much smaller horse. The late afternoon sun struck silver on the man's saddle. Calistro! By the Lord, it was Calistro!

Van Buskirk trotted back to his horse. When he came past the camp, the dun ran, whickering, around the corral and then it paused before the barrier, as if ready to crash through and follow Van Buskirk.

Damn a pet horse. Squanto had said the dun followed McQuiston and Calistro like a dog. They must have their own way of making it stay in a flimsy corral, but Van Buskirk knew only one method. He couldn't have the thing trotting along with him when he went after Calistro.

He unloosed one of the corral ropes, and tied the dun to a tree. It stood trembling, backing slowly away from the rope.

Van Buskirk went after Calistro.

Coming to the first of the open hills, Van Buskirk found that he had almost overrun the Mexican. Calistro was riding leisurely. By sundown, Van Buskirk thought he had everything figured out. Calistro was going straight to the Y. McQuiston, who had been warned not to go to the dance, was going anyway; and his Mexican friend would meet him there.

Much later, Van Buskirk was puzzled when Calistro stopped, unsaddled his horse, and settled down behind a hill that overlooked the Y. With the patience of a man who knows he has the advantage, Van Buskirk waited.

Two men in a light rig jounced up the road and stopped at the Darland place. Grandma Varnum talked to them from the porch, and then they unharnessed and put their horse into the corral. Not long afterward Van Buskirk saw Evaleth and Dan and Mark Copperwhaite racing the last quarter of a mile to the Y.

Completely absorbed for a time, grinning, Van Buskirk watched the race. The two brothers beat their sister by fifty yards.

The after-glow of sunset faded behind the steep hills across the river from the Y. Van Buskirk peered from the brush on the edge of a wash, watching Calistro, who did not seem concerned about anything below. It was irritating.

Just before dusk McQuiston came.

Van Buskirk watched June run from the house to greet him. They stood beside the bay for a few moments and McQuiston gave her something. Van Buskirk compressed his lips. June walked to the corral with McQuiston, and then they were close together when they went back to the house, both making a fuss over something she held.

Darkness came. Troy Clinton's violin music sounded thinly. Van Buskirk's false patience was strained. He no longer knew where Calistro was.

He built up a fine anger. Here he was missing the dance, and Squanto and Teague wouldn't appreciate what he was doing, even if he saved one of them from being strangled by a rawhide rope.

The hill was dark and silent. Evening chill ran up the wash. All at once Van Buskirk remembered the dismal rain on the day they hanged Max Roby; he cursed the fact that such a thought should pop up unasked.

CHAPTER 8

June ran from the house to greet McQuiston. "You did come, after all!"

"I just happened to be riding this way, so—"

"You did not! You came purposely, didn't you?"

"Well, you invited me, and since I was going by anyway—"

"You came purposely, didn't you?"

June's insistence tugged at the wary side of McQuiston's mind. Her eyes kept probing for his answer, as if she wanted to grab it to her and gloat over it; but the rest of her expression was anxious, radiant, as though she needed desperately to be accepted and assured. McQuiston knew he had never seen a face of such clear purity.

He was ashamed of his brief doubting. He grinned and said, quite honestly, "Yes, I've been thinking of coming here all week." He swung down and gave her the kitten.

"It's a beautiful little thing, Mr. McQuiston!"

"My name is Dallas. And don't make it 'Uncle Dallas' either."

They laughed at Squanto's expense, standing close together beside the horse. June held the kitten in both hands, rubbing her cheek against it. She went to the corral with McQuiston, waiting while he took care of the bay.

"Grandma Varnum cussed under her breath when she saw you turn in. She's afraid there'll be trouble."

"I hope not." McQuiston looked at the horses in the corral. "You must have a crowd already."

"Two mining engineers who stop here now and then, Evaleth Copperwhaite and two of her brothers—that's all. Have you ever seen Evaleth?"

"I met her on the road one day."

"She's pretty, isn't she?"

"She had a good looking horse, I remember."

June laughed. "You're hard to pin down, I can see." On the way to the house she asked, "Did you look at Buffalo Meadows?"

"Yes. I filed right up the middle of the park."

"Good!" June held the cat tightly against her cheek. "We're neighbors now."

The engineers were two young men named Wilson and Koering. They were helping Grandma Varnum cut up chickens to be fried for the midnight supper. They gave McQuiston damp handshakes and friendly grins.

Mark and Dan Copperwhaite were tall lads, all gangling arms and legs, with big hands and great manes of sandy hair that had been soaked down before combing.

Mark, the younger of the two, acknowledged McQuiston's greeting stiffly.

McQuiston remembered where he had seen the two before, at the schoolhouse the first day he and Calistro were on the Tumbling.

"And Evaleth—" June looked around with a little frown. "Where's Evaleth? She was here just a second ago."

Evaleth Copperwhaite came from one of the bedrooms a few moments later, timing her entrance perfectly to meet the momentary interest in her absence. There was a delicate tone of irritation in June's voice when she presented Evaleth. "My dearest friend. She's the tomboy of the country."

"I must say you don't look it, Miss Copperwhaite." She was taller than McQuiston had thought. Lamplight heightened her golden coloring and hid the sun streaks in her hair. Her eyes were long, Scotch-flecked, her mouth wide and strong, with humor latent at the corners. McQuiston knew she had not ridden here in the pink plaid gingham dress she was wearing. He thought, *If her old man knew where she was, there'd be hell to pay.*

"Where's your friend tonight, Mr. McQuiston?" Evaleth asked.

"He's up at the meadows."

"Buffalo Meadows?" Evaleth was startled. She glanced quickly at June.

"You're hungry," June said. She took McQuiston's arm and led him back to the kitchen, where Grandma Varnum's helpers had just finished their chores.

"Here's a man who hasn't had anything to eat since

breakfast, Grandma Varnum," June said.

"Fix him a dose of poison then." The old woman threw a cloth over pieces of chicken in a pan. She glared at McQuiston and walked into the living room. Troy Clinton came through the front door with his violin, head downcast, shuffling pigeon-toed across the floor and out of McQuiston's vision.

McQuiston was eating when the dance began. Mark Copperwhaite by then had taken June away. Grandma Varnum returned to the kitchen. "So you had to come prodding for trouble, McQuiston."

"I'm a neighbor now."

"What do you mean?"

"I've taken up a slice of Buffalo Meadows."

Grandma Varnum sat down. "Well, by God!"

"Did I make a mistake?"

"You know what you did. Don't try to pump me. Who'd you talk to about it?"

"Charlie Nye."

"He'd give you the straight of it, yes. But he can't help you none, you idiot."

"I didn't ask for help."

"You wouldn't." Grandma Varnum scowled. She pointed a long forefinger at McQuiston. "Do they know about it?" She tipped her head up-river.

"I don't think so. Not yet."

"Not yet is right." Grandma Varnum was hard as flint. "You've deliberately tied yourself to two kinds of grief, McQuiston. The trouble over the meadows is your own. The hell you might get into here is something else. I'll expect decent behavior from you tonight."

She was angry and she was scared, McQuiston knew; and she was thinking of June. "You'll get it," he said.

"I know your kind. Tell them they can't have something and that's just what they go after. You came here tonight for no better reason than that, damn your hide!" Grandma Varnum rose and went into the living room.

She was partly right. McQuiston knew the deviltry in him that bristled the instant he thought he was being affronted. But Buffalo Meadows had been in his mind even before he knew everything about it; and he was attracted to June more strongly than he had ever been to any woman, and not entirely because three men had warned him to stay away from her.

He had a right to compete for anything with Squanto and the others.

June went past the door, dancing with Koering. Her glance said she was displeased with the way McQuiston was still idling over coffee. He watched Evaleth go by with Dan, the skirt of her long dress awhirl.

Grandma Varnum was listening for the heavy tramp of feet on the porch. She was at the door before anyone knocked. Squanto, hat in his hands, seemed to block the whole opening. Grandma Varnum motioned him back, stepped out with him and closed the door, and for an instant there had been a break in Clinton's music.

The old woman brought Squanto straight into the kitchen a few minutes later. He looked down at McQuiston with a massive sort of interest, and McQuiston thought of the story of him lifting a horse with his legs. It was probably true.

"We've agreed it would do June no good to have

trouble here," Grandma Varnum said.

McQuiston nodded. "I didn't bring any with me."

Squanto's mouth showed a touch of humor. The size of him, the powerful look of his hands and wrists, the way he stood with mountainous patience, awed McQuiston for a moment. "Good enough," Squanto said.

When he was turning sidewise to follow Grandma Varnum through the doorway, Squanto said, "I'll try to take Avery and Billy in hand when they get here, Grandma."

"Do that." The old woman's voice was sharp with worry.

McQuiston was standing by the fireplace when Teague came in. The man was all smoothness and a flashing smile, until his eyes snagged on McQuiston. For an instant Teague's manner broke then and McQuiston saw deep into the breach, fury commingled with surprise.

He'll never be satisfied, McQuiston thought, *until he knows what would have happened that day he tried to make a pistol fight.*

Squanto rolled his head toward the kitchen. He took Teague there for a talk.

The two men returned to the living room not long afterward and both seemed to be in good humor. McQuiston watched Teague dancing with Grandma Varnum. The man was courtly, smiling, nodding agreeably to something the old lady was telling him.

McQuiston wondered idly if the old tale that most cold-blooded pistolmen were sandy-complexioned and blond was true.

He danced twice with Evaleth. Maybe she did have tomboyish ways but he was quite aware that she was a desirable woman. "What's your father going to say about this?" he asked.

"He thinks I'm somewhere else."

"But your mother knows?"

"Of course," Evaleth said. "You're smarter than you look, Mr. McQuiston."

They were laughing at the end of the dance, but Evaleth was serious when she said, "You'd better dance with June. I'm afraid she's losing patience with you."

"She's not short of partners."

"You came here to see her, not me." Evaleth looked across the room at Teague.

"I'll get around to her."

"You think well of yourself, don't you, Mr. McQuiston?" Evaleth said. "But if you want to avoid trouble, I'd think you'd better pay June some attention."

McQuiston was not sure that he understood.

Later, watching Clinton as he scraped the strings of his violin, McQuiston decided that things were going to be all right. The fiddler at a dance could often spot the temper of affairs better than anyone else, and Clinton showed nothing to indicate that he saw trouble. McQuiston saw the old man's sour face lighten as his eyes followed June around the room.

"Did Clinton work for June's father in the park?" McQuiston asked of Mark Copperwhaite.

"What?" The youth showed his dislike of McQuiston.

"Clinton. Did he work for Darland?"

"He worked for Roby—and then he stayed on with

79

June," Mark answered curtly. His eyes went back to June.

McQuiston danced just once with June before the trouble started. She said, "You've certainly tried to keep away from me tonight. Why'd you come here at all?"

"I haven't had a chance to get near you."

"You've managed all right with Evaleth."

"Maybe she isn't as popular as you." Neither the heavy compliment nor the smile relaxed the tight look on June's face. *A demanding little devil.* She would never pout or sulk; she'd throw things around and raise hell when a man displeased her. The thought tickled McQuiston.

Grandma Varnum edged up to him after the dance. "I wish you'd leave."

McQuiston stared at her in honest puzzlement. He looked around the room. Squanto was dancing with Evaleth, grinning, having a good time. Teague was dancing with June, smiling. "I don't see any reason to—"

"I wish you'd leave, McQuiston."

Koering came bouncing up with a boyish grin. "You promised me, sweetheart!" He broke up the conversation, and he did not observe Grandma Varnum's worried expression as he danced away with her.

McQuiston looked at Clinton. The old rider was watching June. He glanced at McQuiston and the sour, wary look returned to his face. Grandma Varnum was right: Trouble was brewing. But McQuiston saw no outward signs of it, other than the quick, veiled glance from Clinton.

McQuiston went into the kitchen for a cup of coffee.

Dancing with June, Teague said, "Why did you let that fellow come back here?"

"He's harmless. He's no worse than the two engineers."

"They're not serious about anything. McQuiston is. He's crazy about you, June."

The woman laughed. "He danced with me once."

"That's plenty."

"He'd be hard to run away, Avery."

"Not if you want him run off. Do you?"

"I didn't say that." June smiled. "You're a wonderful dancer, Avery. Squanto is so slow and Billy wants to jump all over the place, but you and McQuiston are different."

"Where he comes from that's all they do."

"Oh? I always heard they do a lot of pistol fighting too. Dallas said—"

"Bragging about it, was he?"

"Well, no, but he said—"

"I don't care what he said." Teague's face was dark. "He didn't mention what happened between us the other day, did he?"

"Not exactly— No he didn't, Avery."

"Yes he did. What was it, bragging about how—"

"No, no!" June shook her head. "Let's forget about it. I wish I hadn't mentioned it." She watched Teague keenly as they passed the doorway to the kitchen. "Can you keep a secret, Avery?"

Teague did not hear at first. June repeated the question and he said, "I'm not Billy Van Buskirk."

"Dallas filed on Buffalo Meadows." June felt the shock, the tightening that went through Teague's whole body. She went on, smiling. "Now there's no sense in making any trouble about it, and besides, you promised Squanto—"

"You're sure of it?"

"Why, yes. He told Evaleth and she told me."

The dance ended. Koering bounded over to June with a grin as soon as Teague escorted her to a chair. She watched Teague staring toward the kitchen. He walked toward the rack near the door where the hats and gun-belts hung.

Squanto seemed to be sauntering, but he covered space quickly as he went toward Teague. He reached out to take Teague by the shoulder and the smaller man jerked his body aside. Teague's face was tight and wickedness was flickering in his eyes as Squanto began to talk.

Clinton struck up another tune quickly. June accepted Koering's hand and rose. She was beautiful and her lips were smiling as she began the dance with the engineer.

McQuiston's brows were dark bars as he stared across the table, through the doorway, and saw it building where the two men were talking near the front door. If there had been whiskey here, it would have been easier to understand.

It was a sharp, fast duel of wills out there in the other room. The music and the feet of the dancers covered everything but Teague's small, quick gestures, the rapid movements of his lips, and the bitter glances he flashed from Squanto to McQuiston. Squanto's back was turned, his body covering one side of Teague, and it was only when Teague shot a vicious look at him that McQuiston knew Squanto had spoken.

Then the two men, with Squanto in front, came straight toward the kitchen. Squanto stopped in the doorway. Without rancor he said, "Beat it, McQuiston."

"So the truce is over?"

"Go on," Squanto said quietly. "Out the back door. I'll bring you your hat and pistol when you're on your horse."

In spite of his calmness Squanto's vitality was an overflowing force in the silence.

"What changed your mind?" McQuiston asked.

Squanto rolled his hand toward the back door. "Go on."

McQuiston did not move.

Teague was trying to crowd past Squanto. "I said the soft way wouldn't work. Let me—"

"It'll work, or I'll slap all the taste out of his mouth right here in the house." Squanto's chest moved with a slow breath. "Get out of here, McQuiston."

McQuiston met the calm stare.

"You can get on your horse by yourself, or I'll put you there." Squanto's arms hung at his sides. There was no anger in his manner. "We can start from here or out in the yard. Now I'm through talking."

McQuiston's reckless spirit surfaced in a grin. "To tell you the truth, the last thing I want to do is go out in the yard with you, but since you've invited me . . . ." He rose and went toward the back door.

Squanto said, "You're going to watch, Teague. That's

83

all, understand?" It was an order and an insult.

McQuiston understood the wrecking of the truce. This was Teague's fight but Squanto was taking it on, doing what he could to protect June, lessening the violence from pistols to fists.

The thought was borne out when Squanto said, "I may be doing you a favor, McQuiston."

McQuiston looked back at the huge shape of the man blotting out the light as he came through the doorway. It was no favor.

Grandma Varnum's protest was an angry wail, "Squanto, you promised me!" There was a lack of decisiveness in her voice, as if she knew she could not forestall this violence as she had before. "Get out in the road!"

They did not go that far. They went around the house and down near a corral. Squanto said cheerfully, "Road, hell. A man could fall over a rock and break a leg out there. Hurry up with that lantern, Dan."

Light streamed from the front door as people rushed out. Dan Copperwhaite came around the house on the run, the lantern in his hand throwing jerky blobs of light. Squanto started to say something to Teague.

McQuiston measured the big man in the uncertain light and hit him as hard as he could in the jaw. He was surprised when Squanto staggered back.

"You fool!" Teague said viciously. "You let him get in the first lick!"

There had to be a weak spot somewhere in any man. McQuiston decided it was Squanto's stomach. He saw white flashes as two blows slid off his head when he was working in, half crouched, to get at Squanto's middle. He slammed his fists four times into Squanto's belly.

It was like beating a tightly filled sack of grain.

Before McQuiston could back away, Squanto smashed him to his knees. McQuiston grabbed Squanto's legs and then his ankles, trying to upset him and gain time to rise without being kicked. He might as well have tugged on a corral post.

Squanto leaned down, grabbed McQuiston under one arm and heaved him to his feet and flung him backward.

"If we're going to fight, let's stay on our feet," Squanto said.

Reeling back, with one arm thrown wide to gain balance, McQuiston crashed into Teague, who shoved against him and steadied him. "Anything to help you get crippled, McQuiston," Teague said. He shoved McQuiston forward.

The belly was not Squanto's weak spot; McQuiston lanced in to try the jaw again. The next instant he was rocking on his back. His mind brought him up while his body was still shocked. Squanto was waiting. McQuiston backed up and looked him over. The man's coolness was more to be feared than his strength, and his strength was incredible.

McQuiston fought then the only way that offered him a chance, staying outside of Squanto's reach, sliding in to strike where he could, absorbing what he could not escape. He was fast and deft for a while. He weighed a hundred and eighty pounds and he pivoted all the weight he could into his blows. But each one of Squanto's post-like jolts jarred a little more power from McQuiston's body.

It could not last long, McQuiston knew. He'd wear himself out in a few more minutes, even if Squanto, a body puncher, didn't raise his sights to catch him in the face. He landed a solid blow on Squanto's jaw. Once more Squanto gave way. McQuiston saw it happen with a dull sense of surprise. The man did have a soft spot, for all his terrible strength.

McQuiston went in to have it over. He caught the big, round jaw again. He was knocked back, gasping, with pain crushing his chest. Again he carried in and struck, and staggered sidewise when Squanto slammed him in the chest. McQuiston went on, past the few minutes he had given himself, although he did not know it.

Squanto was a great bulk with no clear edges, always waiting, a monster of the uncertain light. He sent dull thuds that exploded exhaustion into McQuiston's being. McQuiston's shoulders ached and his legs burned with weariness. He used the leverage of his body, wheeling power to the ends of his fists. His mind sent the blows savagely, but their force was waning.

He saw Squanto's head go back. Squanto was close to the corral poles then, and McQuiston wondered hazily how he had got there. Out of the blurry shadows of punishment McQuiston grasped the fact that he had stood up to this giant. He saw Squanto's head rock back under another smash and then roll tiredly, as if the man could no longer exercise sharp control over it.

Why, if I can stay on my feet, I can do it, McQuiston thought.

He drove his shoulder against Squanto and forced him against the corral poles. McQuiston hit the jaw again. He saw Squanto's head droop. McQuiston braced his hand against the other man's chest, pushing back to get room for one last punch.

With almost the last of his strength McQuiston sent the blow. At the same instant Squanto sagged away, collapsing to a sitting position. McQuiston's fist struck a corral pole. There was little pain at first. He fell against the rails, spraddled over Squanto, clawing bark to keep erect.

Squanto made a gusty, shuddering sound deep in his chest. He tried to push up and could not do it.

There was no elation in McQuiston, no sense of victory; he was too nearly done. He turned slowly. The lanterns gave light that expanded and contracted weirdly. Two lanterns now. He wondered vaguely where the second one had come from. Shadowy forms moved before him. A face grew larger than the rest and it was Teague's.

"That's a start," Teague said. "Try me now."

A man cursed in a shocked tone. A woman's voice, far away it seemed, protested.

McQuiston lowered his head, blinking, when a haziness drifted between him and Teague. He pushed away from the corral. The pain in his hand was suddenly white and screaming. He wanted to rub the hand but he dared not; he couldn't let Teague know it was hurt. "Come ahead," McQuiston mumbled, and lurched toward Teague.

The rope was soundless, a thin streak snaking across

the light from the lanterns the Copperwhaites held. A loop fell around Teague's neck. His hands moved like the front paws of a cat the instant the rawhide touched him. Before the rope could tighten to sear his throat he was trying to haul in slack.

On the rim of the night beyond the lanterns Ben Calistro said, "Hold tight, but do not fight a man already beaten."

The lanterns jerked toward the sound of his voice. The light showed him standing ready to pull in slack in case Teague rushed toward him. Teague did not try it; the loop around his neck was too small already. He strained against the rope with his hands, and his face was ghastly, as if he were fighting off a hangman's noose.

At the corner of the corral a shadow grew behind Calistro. It came in a rush, a rifle glinting in an upraised arm. Calistro made a half turn but Van Buskirk was upon him too soon. The rifle slashed down. There was a thud as Calistro fell. Slack dropped into the rope and Teague flung the loop off his neck.

"There, by God!" Van Buskirk said. "I'll show him how a rope around the neck feels!" He began to drag in the reata. "I've waited half the night to get at him."

Van Buskirk had all the attention for a few moments and then the interest shifted. Evaleth Copperwhaite came running from the porch. "That man has been beaten enough!"

"Not nearly enough," Teague said.

Dan grabbed his sister's arm as she ran past him. He dragged her back, shaking his head. "No, Ev, this is none of our business."

Light on his feet and fast, Teague wheeled and cracked his fist into McQuiston's face. "You haven't even begun to have enough, my friend."

For a while McQuiston tried to fight, and thought he was still fighting. He kept staggering ahead, lashing out at a face he never touched. He dragged on, making movements, trying, but his efforts were no more than that. Blows hammered him. He could not smash the face floating before him in the red mists.

He went down. Teague began to kick him. Evaleth cried out her scorn and Teague paid no attention. Her brothers looked uneasily at each other. At last Dan said, "You'll kill him, Teague!"

"I mean to." The point of Teague's boot struck McQuiston's neck again.

Van Buskirk had put the rope around Calistro's neck, but he had done no more. Calistro was unconscious, there was no attention on Van Buskirk now, and he felt that somehow he had been cheated out of his full revenge. He stared at Teague, and the man's raw savagery appalled him. Van Buskirk felt the same darkly hideous sensations of the day they had hanged Roby. He yelled hoarsely, "That's enough, Teague!"

Teague swung his boot again. There was a blankness in his expression. He drew back his foot and kicked once more. McQuiston was inert, face down.

June was alone on the porch during the last of the fight, after Evaleth had run out to protest. The kitten in June's hands let out a tormented mew. She held it tighter, staring across the yard when Teague was beating McQuiston down.

The kitten struggled. It gave a tortured squall. June's fingers tightened harder. McQuiston went down. The kitten's claws raked June's wrist. Her hands clenched hard. Breathing through her mouth, her eyes wide with fascination, she watched Teague's flashing boots.

The sodden thumps of leather against flesh came back to her like drum beats rising toward incredible excitement. Her lands began to twist, to crush.

CHAPTER 9

It was Squanto who stopped the punishment. He got on his feet, rocking like a drunken man. He shambled forward and knocked Teague sidewise with his shoulder. "What are you doing?" Squanto growled. He was like a wounded grizzly as he stood there swaying, glaring at Teague. "What are you trying to do?"

Teague started in again. Van Buskirk shouted angrily at him. Squanto drew his arm back to strike. Teague stopped. He looked around slowly and comprehension flooded over the blankness of his expression. He rubbed his arm across his forehead. "I guess I lost my temper."

He walked away quickly into the darkness.

Koering and Wilson were on the verge of expressing their opinions of the night's savagery, but Troy Clinton, his violin under one arm, touched Wilson's elbow and nodded toward the bunkhouse. The engineers walked away with the old man.

Evaleth started to go over to McQuiston. Dan pulled her back and turned her toward the house. "Go change your clothes, Ev, while we're saddling up."

"But—"

"Go on!"

For a few moments longer Squanto stood where he was, looking down at McQuiston, and then he rolled his shoulders and went toward the corral. He and Teague rode away shortly afterward, but not together.

Calistro moved. Van Buskirk started to jerk the rope and then he observed that Calistro was still out, his motion only a loose struggle toward consciousness. Van Buskirk dropped the rope. He took Calistro's pistol and flung it toward the house.

Dan said, "Go saddle the horses, Mark." Dan bent over McQuiston.

"The end of a fine evening," Van Buskirk grumbled. No one had given him any attention. He felt robbed of his victory. His horse was still up on the hillside, added inconvenience to a day that had gone sour.

He strode off to find his horse.

At the foot of the steps Evaleth jumped when she stepped on something soft and yielding. She picked up June's kitten. For one shocked instant she thought she had crushed it, but when she held it to the light of the windows, her face twisted at what she saw and she knew she had not done that.

June was sitting on the top step. Evaleth held the scrap of fur toward her. "Your poor little kitten . . ."

"The kitten?" June's voice was dreamy. It grew sharp suddenly. "Oh! One of the men stepped on it!"

"I suppose," Evaleth said uncertainly. She laid the dead kitten on the edge of the porch. As she leaned over she saw a line of scratches on June's wrist and a bit of fur clinging to the cuff of her dress.

"Are those two hurt bad?" June asked.

"I don't know." Evaleth hesitated on the porch, staring down at June, and then she ran into the house with a strange terror chasing her.

The full light of the room was welcome. Grandma Varnum was sitting in a straight-backed chair, stubbornly facing away from the windows. She said harshly, "Well, did they manage to kill each other?"

The kitten . . . It had come mewing along the porch when she and June were standing there, and June had picked it up, and she had been holding it when Evaleth ran into the yard to cry out against Teague's brutality.

"Are you deaf?" Grandma Varnum said. "I asked you if they managed to kill each other."

"They tried to." Evaleth hesitated, biting her lip, thinking about the kitten. "Yes, they—I'm going home."

"I heard you trying to stop it. A waste of time. As far as I'm concerned—" Grandma Varnum studied Evaleth's face. "What's the matter—haven't you ever seen men fight before?"

"Not like that." Evaleth hurried toward the bedroom to change her clothes. On her way out, with her brothers already waiting with the horses, she paused beside Grandma Varnum. "Are you—are you going to stay here?"

"Tonight, at least," the old woman answered. "What's ailing you, Ev?"

"Nothing. Good-night."

Only Calistro and McQuiston were left when

Grandma Varnum rose at last and went out on the porch. June was sitting on the top step. Out in the yard, the two lanterns were still burning. Immense shadows jerked across the light as Calistro helped McQuiston to his feet, guiding him to the water trough near the hill spring.

"I ought to go help them," June said.

"Stay here." Grandma Varnum was grim. "You've helped enough for one night." On her way across the yard she kicked Calistro's pistol and stopped to pick it up.

Muted talk came from near the trough. Grandma Varnum was grinding out an opinion in an angry tone. Calistro's voice made soft sounds in Spanish, and once he laughed. June heard McQuiston say, "I'll live."

After a while Clinton and the two engineers came from the bunkhouse. Clinton scuffed across the yard, going to the corral, and then he returned with McQuiston's horse. June heard McQuiston say, "Just leave me alone. I'll make it." But he could not mount by himself. The engineers and Clinton and Calistro were all in a tight group, boosting McQuiston into the saddle.

He clung to the horn, hunched over. Calistro led the horse away.

Grandma Varnum came across the yard with one of the lanterns. June was crying over the dead kitten. The oily fumes of coal oil were strong when Grandma Varnum blew the lantern out.

Her voice was harsh. "What happened to the little tom?"

"Somebody stepped on it."

"That's too bad. Come on inside, June. I want to talk to you."

"I never had a pet of any kind. I was always afraid of saddle horses. The kitten was so warm and furry and now . . ." June went on crying.

"Put it down and come inside."

When they were in the house Grandma Varnum did not speak her mind at once. She stirred around the room, blowing out lamps, kicking embers back into the fireplace, looking glumly at heavy furniture that must be moved back into place. With mixed belligerence and uncertainty she kept watching June's tear streaked face.

At last. the old lady made her accusation. "And what caused all the trouble?"

"I did," June said in a low voice. "It was all my fault."

Worked up for a strong outburst, Grandma Varnum lost steam before she was well started. All set for resistance, she found none and so she tried to create her own opposition. "Of course it was all your fault! They weren't friendly by no means but they were getting along until you went to work on Teague. I saw what you were up to. What did you do, tell him about the meadows?"

"No." June was humble, penitent.

"You told him plenty, whatever it was! You know all you have to do is flip your finger at him or Billy to make them wild. Squanto is different, but Teague is about half ready to kill somebody all the time. You played on that and don't deny it!"

June's head was bowed. "Yes, it was my fault."

"Why'd you do it, Junie? Why?"

"Dallas danced with Evaleth all the time. He made a fool of himself over her."

Again Grandma Varnum was robbed of opposition, for she had been about to accuse June of the very thing the woman had admitted. "Maybe he was trying to be decent, trying to avoid trouble. Did you ever think of that?"

"I did, but it was too late then. I know I was wrong, Grandma."

Grandma Varnum kept flailing, even though she knew she was defeated. "Squanto did the best he could. I'll say that for him. He took a killing off your hands, and look what he got out of his efforts."

"How did Dallas look?"

"Like a piece of steak!" Grandma Varnum said bitterly. "What do you expect when two brutes like that slam into each other?"

June stared at the floor, a picture of misery.

"You've got to get settled down, girl. You can't have men coming here, fighting over you, making people think you're a—" Grandma Varnum hesitated "—a bad woman. That won't do at all."

June ran to the old woman and clung to her, sobbing. "I love him, Grandma."

"Who? That big McQuiston lout?"

"Yes! I love him."

Grandma Varnum rolled her eyes at the ceiling. "You've seen him two times!"

"I don't care. I know what I think."

It struck Grandma Varnum hard. That was the way it had been when she first saw Jim. She had talked to him a few minutes, danced with him once, and had known then that he was the only man for her. Grandma Varnum had a fear that age would do to her what she had seen it do to others, make them forget, make them believe things which were easily tailored from the sentimental mists of time to fit a popular notion.

She abhorred the thought of such a softening in herself and so she leaned hard the other way; but she knew her mind had not betrayed her. It was no frothy dream about loving Jim Varnum the first time she laid eyes on him. So now she had no ground from which to criticize June.

"You've got to be sure, June. He may be no good. Because he ain't afraid of other men—that don't mean a thing. Maybe he's a drifter who won't last until snow flies. Any man can fight. They do that from the time they can lift their arms. But we'll let him hang around—"

"But if he comes here the others will kill him."

"I don't hardly think so, Junie. You saw what Squanto did tonight. He ain't afraid of McQuiston and neither is Billy." The old woman hesitated. "Teague is. Teague would kill him if he could."

"How can you tell those things?" June asked. No longer crying, she walked over to the fireplace.

"When it comes to men, I've seen enough—I think I can tell a few things," Grandma Varnum said. She sat down. Her body was tired. She wished she were home, but still she wanted to help June solve her troubles. McQuiston might be the answer after all. If June really loved him, the two of them wouldn't need much help from Grandma Varnum.

Where June would need help was in handling the

others. Maybe I can give her some advice, Grandma Varnum thought. Advice. What was that worth to young people in love? The old woman looked over at June. *I wonder if she thinks I'm an old busy-body? Maybe she laughs behind my back, and me thinking I'm still some use in the world.*

"You did tell me the truth tonight, June—you didn't tell Teague about McQuiston and the meadows?"

"Evaleth told him."

"Hmm. No wonder she acted so scared when she came in here after it was all over." Grandma Varnum shook her head. "I always liked that girl."

"I did too. She tried to stop the fight. You've got to remember that."

"Yeah. Start a landslide and then throw a stick at it to prove you ain't guilty." Grandma Varnum rose. "I'm going to bed. This room can go to hell for straightening up tonight. I wouldn't have thought that of Ev."

"Why don't you stay here with me all the time?"

"Too much of a bustle," Grandma Varnum said. "But I'll try to be around when you need me."

CHAPTER 10

Calistro went up the hill to get his horse, leaving McQuiston in the road. Calistro had known Van Buskirk was trailing him but when the Mexican made his last move to the barn on foot he thought perhaps he had lost Van Buskirk, at least for a time. Calistro shrugged it off. One could not win always.

He found his pony and went back to the road.

McQuiston had fallen out of the saddle and was sitting with his head on his knees.

"Shall we go back to the ranch?" Calistro asked.

"No. Let's go on home."

"Ah, yes, home." Calistro helped McQuiston mount again. It took effort and when it was done, Calistro's headache was even larger than before. "We will go slowly."

It was quite slow. McQuiston did not fall out of the saddle again, but several times he had to slide down to rest. Two times Calistro built a fire and sat looking solemnly at his partner. McQuiston was very tough, like a *ladino* steer that could be spilled end over end in the worst of the *brasada,* and then rise to run full speed again.

In this *gringo* country it was frowned upon to kick a man after he was beaten down, but of course that was a way to make sure he did not rise again. Brutality could rouse no terrible resentment in Benevides Calistro because he had seen much of it. Perhaps kicking was considered bad here, but men did not like a rope around their necks either.

At each fire stop McQuiston rested long, rousing each time to say, "What are we doing here?" And then he had to be helped upon his horse again.

It was daylight when they came to the camp near the park.

Calistro looked calmly at the little dun that had never known a rope. Someone had tied it to a tree. In its struggle to be free the horse had broken the rope but it had become entangled in the other ropes and the snaggy logs of the corral and now it was dead, with no fatal mark upon it except terror.

"Van Buskirk," Calistro said. "He is the one."

McQuiston lay down on his blankets and closed his eyes.

Calistro kept looking at the horse. They would do something about this. There was much to be done later. Perhaps, even, they should do something about the dead man he had found in the rocks on the other side of the ridge, although there was nothing one could do to help a dead man.

He began to untangle the wreckage of the corral. He used McQuiston's horse to drag the dun to the mouth of the gulch, far away from the camp.

McQuiston was feeling much better after two days, although he had to be careful about moving certain muscles quickly. His face was not badly marked but his body was stiff and sore from the pounding he had taken. On the third day he and Calistro went to meet the wagon McQuiston had hired in Columbine. The teamster was on time and they escorted him to Buffalo Meadows.

They set up in the cabin, Calistro no longer voicing objections about staying there.

"It's time to see about some cows," McQuiston said.

Calistro looked out upon the meadows. "About the dun? What—"

McQuiston said, "Van Buskirk owes us a horse. We'll get it."

"And if they come here to scare us away?"

"We'll fight. They ought to know it by now."

Calistro nodded. "And you will go again to the

woman's ranch when it pleases you?"

"Yes."

"We will stay on this land the five years?"

"I'm for it," McQuiston said. "How about you?"

"At first I did not like it, but it is a good place and I am content to stay. Much is settled then. There is one small thing I did not speak of."

"What's that, Ben?"

As if speaking of the weather, Calistro said, "There is a dead man here. Perhaps we should bury him."

The bluish-green flesh around McQuiston's eyes gathered in little puckers.

"In the rocks over the ridge." Calistro pointed. "It is not a place where one would ride." He raised his brows. "If you wish we do not have to go near him. He will be no worse because of that."

"How come you ran onto him?"

"After camping, I made all the ground of the ridge well known to me. That is always good to do." Calistro shrugged. "And so I found him."

"Tell me about him."

"What is there to say about a dead man?"

"How long had he been there?" McQuiston asked.

"Since he died, I would say." Calistro's smile was partly mockery and partly amusement. "A year, two years . . . Who can say?"

"There was a man named Corbett who disappeared from here. Was there anything around the body to tell—"

"I did not go very close. He was dead. I could do nothing to help him, no matter who he was."

"That's true, but let's go have another look."

The remains were not skeletal, but more like those of a sun-dried cadaver, lying in a small pocket among tumbled rocks. McQuiston walked in down-wind. The rotting clothes were the average garb of any man who might ride the hills. The boots had been much more expensive than the rest of the clothes, beautifully stitched, with inlaid four-leaf clovers.

McQuiston picked up a .45 Colt revolver that might have fallen from the holster when the man spilled down from the higher rocks, where Calistro was now sitting, the forward pitched position of the body indicating that there must have been a fall. The pistol was fully loaded, the edges of the cases showing green corrosion.

"What do you know of him now?" Calistro asked.

McQuiston shook his head. "He had a good pistol and good boots."

"In the pockets, maybe something to tell—"

"I'm not that interested," McQuiston said.

"Then we can bury him and go away?"

"No. A man disappeared up here. This may be him. We'll send word to the sheriff."

"Sheriffs make trouble, ask questions, discover nothing," Calistro said. "Do we need a sheriff up here?"

"Yeah." McQuiston shoved the pistol under his belt. They went back to the cabin. At the upper end of the meadows a buggy was coming with a rider beside it.

Calistro said, "It is the woman, with someone."

"Her name is June, damn it."

"It is June," Calistro said. When she arrived he was

101

nailing poles at the corner of the corral most removed from the cabin.

Bill Minot was the man with June, the second half of her riding crew. He was a wrinkled little man in his late fifties. It was obvious that he had been brought along as a chaperon, and he was not happy about it. "The meadows look good," he said glumly. "Range was good up where I been all summer, too." He went down to the corral to talk to Calistro.

June looked into the cabin. "Oh, you've fixed it up!"

"Roughly," McQuiston said. "It's not like when you lived here, I imagine."

"I remember getting up in the mornings in the summer. The sun would be just coming over the tops of those trees, and I would run and run along the edge of the meadow, trying to meet it, until I was clear down there where the fence turns." June gave McQuiston a quick, child-like smile. "Did you ever do anything silly like that when you were little?"

"I've been running to meet the sun all my life," McQuiston said. "I know what you mean."

The woman studied his expression intently. "I think you do. You're the first person I ever talked to who understood what I meant—except my father. He understood. He wouldn't let my mother scold me when I came back late for breakfast."

"You thought a lot of your father, didn't you?"

"Yes. Even more now when I'm old enough to look back and understand."

"I never saw my father." Oliver McQuiston had been a soldier-of-fortune in South America, in Mexico, and he had been killed when his son was a few days old. McQuiston's mother was only a shifting memory of soft, laughing eyes, of murmuring, of warmth. She had died before his remembrance was solidly established.

"Why was—" McQuiston started to ask why Fred Darland was killed, but he changed his mind and said, "Why didn't your father prove up on this place, June?"

"When my mother died, he couldn't stand it up here any more. He didn't want the place after that." June turned and looked at the great meadows rippling in the wind. "But I still love it. I'd like to come back here someday, away from the river where everybody—"

When she did not finish, McQuiston said, "Where everyone is unfriendly?"

"No, they're not. It's mostly my fault, I suppose. Things like last Saturday."

"That wasn't your fault," McQuiston said. "I shouldn't have gone there."

"But I asked you to!" June watched him steadily. "You're not going to stay away now, are you?"

"I'm a brute for punishment." McQuiston grinned. "I'll be back."

"When?"

"Don't rush me. Ben and me still have lots of things to straighten out up here." He frowned at the meadows. "How come no one ever ran cows here after your father moved?"

"Squanto and the others wouldn't let anyone in here. They ran everyone off. You won't let them do that to you though, will you?"

"Well," McQuiston said, "we'll get around to that

when the time comes." He looked to where Calistro and Minot were squatted at the corner of the corral, talking like old friends. "Do you remember any man around the country who had a pair of boots with green four-leaf clovers?"

The woman held the question a long time. "Why?"

"Nothing much." A man might notice such boots; it was doubtful that a woman would.

"Why?" June asked.

"It was just an idea."

"No," June said quietly. "Why did you ask about Len Corbett's boots?"

"Len Corbett? You're sure?"

"I danced with him at the Y. He was there twice after he filed on Buffalo Meadows. What about him, Dallas?"

"Calistro found him."

"Where?"

"Over in the rocks."

"What—How—" June moistened her lips slowly. "How was he killed?"

"He might have fallen. Maybe his horse threw him. It—I couldn't tell you."

"His horse didn't throw him," June said. "Rodney Varnum bought that sorrel from the county, and his kids have been riding it, three and four at a time, ever since. How was Corbett killed, Dallas?"

McQuiston shook his head.

"What did you do with him?"

"Nothing. When we have time we'll send word to the sheriff. It was only a while ago—today—that I knew about it."

"You mean Calistro found him several days ago, and just let him lie there?" June thinned her lips.

"How long ago did he disappear?"

"About a year ago."

"What could Ben have done for him—now?"

"Let's go over there," June said.

"Good Lord, June!" McQuiston shook his head.

"Let's go over there. I want to be sure. How far can we get in the buggy?"

"Not very far. All there is to tell about is those boots, and you already know about them."

"Len Corbett had some gold caps on his teeth, in the back of his mouth," June said. "Get a tarpaulin. I'll take the buggy as far as I can and we'll bring him back in it."

"The sheriff gets paid for that," McQuiston protested. He went into the cabin and came back with the pistol he had picked up. "Do you remember—"

"I couldn't tell one pistol from another. Get some canvas, Dallas."

All four of them went in the buggy. June got it much farther than McQuiston had thought she could. In fact, her fast turns against cramped front wheels made him nervous. They went the last two hundred yards on foot.

June peered closely at the body. McQuiston and Minot looked at each other uncomfortably. Calistro began to shake out the canvas, his face showing its usual tinge of bitter humor.

"It's Corbett," June said.

McQuiston looked inquiringly at Minot. The old rider shook his head. "I never saw the man. I spend most of my time in cow camp." He began to help Calistro.

Back at the cabin, June said, "Bill and I will take him down to the river and send word to the sheriff."

Minot's gloomy expression indicated that he shared Calistro's attitude: The hills were full of bones like these; they would have saved trouble by burying the man and telling the sheriff when it came handy, if it ever did.

June touched McQuiston's arm. "I'm sorry about arguing with you, but it's only decent that any man should be buried properly, instead of having a few rocks thrown over him. My own father—" She shook her head and went toward the buggy.

McQuiston gave her a hand up. "Sure, that's the right thing to do."

He watched the buggy leave. The way June drove worried him. On a sideling place like Squire's Hill it would be easy to flip a light rig before the driver knew what was happening. He turned to look at Calistro, but Calistro had already gone back to the corral and was picking up his hammer.

I have said nothing. But Calistro's unspoken thoughts were stronger than words. He was probably thinking that June had shown an unseemly fascination with death. It appeared so, but McQuiston built against the thought. He knew from Dan Copperwhaite the story of Fred Darland's death.

The sheriff had looked at him and ordered him buried at once, almost where he lay. That was man logic and understandable, but to June and her sisters it must have seemed indecent and unfeeling, so now June did not want to have such an act repeated, no matter who the man.

McQuiston satisfied himself. He went down where Calistro was working and began to help him. After a while the Mexican said, "There is the matter of the horse and Van Buskirk."

"We'll collect," McQuiston said. "But first, don't you think we ought to wait and see what's going to happen right here?"

"Perhaps, yes." Calistro gave the matter some thought. "If it is the way of the one called Squanto, we will wait a long time, wondering every day, so long that it will seem nothing is going to happen—and then it will."

"That's Squanto, all right."

"If it is the way of the other two, they will be here now, tomorrow, soon." Calistro spread his hands. "I do not wish to be dragged across the grass."

"We don't want to be found like Corbett, either."

"Then we both have worries." Calistro smiled. "But when we first saw the meadows, our minds guessed certain things, and we are still here."

McQuiston was truly Mexican in the way he accepted the situation. There was no defense that could be set up. He said, "When they come, they will come, and we will be here." He thought it unlikely that Squanto could bear his waiting patience on hot-tempered men like Teague and Van Buskirk for any great length of time.

CHAPTER 11

Squanto Whitcomb's life was based on order, which was reflected in the buildings of his ranch, in the way he used his range, and in his dealings with other men. He was one of an Ohio family of fourteen children. The eight brothers were all such individuals that by the time they were half grown, although they were seldom in violent opposition, they simply could not get along with each other, and so they had gone in the particular direction that suited each one.

At eighteen Squanto was a Union infantry private. At twenty-one, due largely to a grasp of order in the midst of one of the most disorderly regiments in the Western Army, and because of remarkable stability under fire, he was a colonel, and greatly disgusted with the waste of war.

The only person who had ever upset the slow, stubborn way of his life was June Darland. He thought he understood her thoroughly, but in spite of that, she still lay in his life so strongly she had caused him to do wasteful and unnecessary acts.

The worst of all had been the hanging of Max Roby.

Rage had caused that, a vice which Squanto seldom indulged in. Ordinarily, before even considering the act that had been done on Los Pinos on a rainy day, Squanto would have ground all the facts fine against reason. But on that day, all he could think of was the frailty of June Darland and the injustice that had been done her.

Brooding over mistakes was another failing Squanto did not allow himself; but he knew he could never get the hanging completely from his mind. It was done. The wonder lay in the fact that a woman could have influenced him enough to have unbalanced his judgment.

In spite of that, Squanto knew that he was going to marry June; there was not even a small grain of doubt in his mind.

He stood now watching progress on the house he was building for her. The foundation of stone was set below frost line in a country where there never was any difficulty over the heaving of the earth in spring. The logs were eighteen inches thick, two years in seasoning. If she wanted white-painted board siding over them, that would be done.

Before fall the walls would be up and the roof shingled. Thereafter, the interior would be done as June directed. She knew nothing of all this, but it did not matter, for Squanto's belief that he and June would be married in time was as solid as the sunny hill against which the house backed.

He watched the men at work. Two of them were mine timbermen, stopped here for two weeks while on their way to Lake City. They were wizards with an adze and broadaxe. The helpers were Squanto's two riders. He knew they should be in the hills now, but that was only a small part of the disruption June had brought into his life.

Squanto was ready now to go to the line camp where his two riders should have been. He was mounting when

Teague and Van Buskirk rode around the shoulder of the hill. The sight of them was enough to know what they had in mind.

Squanto swung out of the stirrup and walked over to the spring from which he would pipe water into the new house. During the minute or two it took for Teague and Van Buskirk to ride up to him, Squanto's mind was on the problem of insulating the water pipe.

The two did not dismount. Van Buskirk said, "Today's as good as any time, Squanto."

"What's the hurry? I've got work to do."

"So have we," Teague said. "So let's get up to the park and finish our business."

"You make it sound easy." Squanto thought of the loss of time from other matters. "They're not going to run from a couple of shots in the air."

"Are you going, or are you going to stall around like you did when Corbett was in the park?" Van Buskirk asked.

"That worked out," Squanto said. "We didn't have to lift a finger, did we?" He gave Teague and Van Buskirk a heavy look. They glanced at each other.

"Stay or go," Teague said. "If you don't go, you're out of the deal for Buffalo Meadows."

"That don't worry me at all." The park was another detour away from a straight way of doing things. None of them really needed it; they could use it, yes, but since McQuiston and Calistro had settled in Buffalo Meadows, Squanto had been weighing the cost of the park against its worth. The price was becoming too high.

"So it doesn't worry you, huh?" Teague put both

hands on the saddle horn and smiled down at Squanto. "June wants the place, no matter how you try to make us think you don't. Shall we let McQuiston give it to her?"

There was the point. Over and over June had told Squanto how much she loved the park and how much she regretted moving from it. Squanto's doubts about her honesty in the matter had been forming slowly for some time; but still, Teague had struck a vital point. Squanto said, "We went too strong with the Shepherds. Let's not—"

"You just got through saying these two won't run from a shot in the air." Teague's smile was stronger now. "What's *your* idea of doing business with them?"

"It ain't murder." Squanto eyed the two men steadily. "Remember Los Pinos?"

"That don't bother me none," Teague said.

Squanto kept watching him. "Don't it?"

Teague shifted in the saddle. "Are you coming or not!"

"Yeah." For another few moments Squanto looked at Teague and then he went to his horse. He was aware of the danger of doing anything reluctantly but that was the way he felt now. The strong habit of common sense told him to let Van Buskirk and Teague have the park, along with the trouble and loss of time the place was costing. But June wanted the land, and whatever she wished, within reason, Squanto would provide.

Van Buskirk grinned as they went past the new house. "I heard of a fellow over in the Saguache country who figured on a big, new place. The old boy had him a pile of bricks burned, big as a haystack. He made plans to

111

patch hell a mile, but he slipped on one little thing. The girl never intended to marry him from the first."

Van Buskirk winked at Teague. "I hear all the chimneys in that whole country since been built out of that pile of brick, and there's still plenty left. What are you building here, Squanto—a stage station or a trading post?"

"A house for me and June," Squanto said.

"She know about it?"

"Not yet." Squanto's attitude was so heavy with simple assurance that Van Buskirk felt like a fool.

And Teague, ever prying under the edges of honesty to find dishonesty, could not discover an answer that suited him. Sometimes Squanto acted like his head was thick, but in stupid oafs there was often the most subtle trickery.

They did not go by way of Squire's Hill, but swung to the east a mile below the hill and followed a deer trail through the aspens, Squanto leading the way. When they approached the basin, Teague called a halt.

He said, "They may be laying for us."

"Sure they might." Squanto took his great weight off the buckskin. He snapped an aspen twig and chewed on it, regarding Teague and Van Buskirk with amusement. "They probably got a fort a mile long, with seven batteries of Parrott rifles." After a while he mounted again and went on.

Where the timber thinned near the edge of the plateau they went on foot until they could see the cabin. Smoke was coming from it. There were at least two horses in the corral. A man came out and picked up an armload of wood and went back inside.

"Settled down like pioneers!" Teague said. "I wouldn't be surprised if they had a garden started. You said their camp was in the timber, Billy."

"It was. What's the plan now, Squanto?"

"We'll ride on down until we're behind the cabin. One man will take the horses back over the hill and stay with them. The other two of us will flank out and work the cabin over with our rifles."

"Those logs!" Teague said. "What good—"

"Let's see what works." Squanto put a hard stare on Teague. "What do *you* want to do—wait until one of them comes out again and knock him over? No, by God. I'm with you about running 'em off, but we didn't come up here to murder."

"Who said anything about murder?" Teague asked angrily. "A bullet through the leg or—"

"Squanto's the boss," Van Buskirk said. "We'll do things his way."

"Fine," Squanto said. "You stay with the horses, Billy."

"Hell no!" Van Buskirk protested. "I didn't come up here to hold horses."

"Me either," Teague said.

Squanto was amused. "All right. We'll stand turns holding the horses, ten minutes at a whack. Billy first."

They went on to a point in the timber from which they could see the back of the cabin. Teague and Squanto took their rifles. Van Buskirk gathered up the reins of the three horses. "Don't nobody forget where I am after ten minutes." He stepped ahead suddenly and tried a pistol shot at the stove pipe of the cabin.

Teague jumped and cursed. Van Buskirk was grinning as he steadied the startled horses and led them away.

For several minutes after he left, Teague and Squanto watched the cabin. They were directly behind it and their view was gently slanting, making the structure appear to merge with the grass. Smoke was drifting from the stove pipe, bending lazily with a wind quartering across the meadows from the east.

Squanto studied Teague critically. The man was tense and excited. He would shoot to kill. Some long delayed conclusions about Avery Teague settled firmly in Squanto's mind.

The two horses below were looking up the hill, but suddenly they seemed to lose interest. They turned and trotted to the lower end of the corral, standing there and looking toward the grass.

Squanto said, "There's no sense in punching a lot of holes in the roof. That's a good cabin."

He and Teague worked out to the sides, losing sight of each other in the timber at once. They were about a hundred and fifty yards apart when they settled down and began to shoot.

McQuiston and Calistro were eating dinner when Van Buskirk's shot sounded on the hill. McQuiston pointed instantly, trusting his first impression to be accurate before after-thinking could confuse the direction. Calistro nodded. They leaped up and buckled on their pistol belts and spilled rifle cartridges into their pockets.

From the edges of the door McQuiston could see only

grass and distant timber. Calistro tried the corners of the windows. He shook his head. McQuiston pointed straight ahead, through the door.

They ran low across the yard and dived into the soggy edge of the first seep beyond the yard. McQuiston expected lead to be driving at them then, but no shots came. They crawled on into the deep grass below the corral.

Two rifles opened up a short time later, the bullets making chunking sounds against the logs of the cabin. The sniper on their right emptied his weapon in a hurry, shooting out the window on that side of the cabin. On the left the fire was slow and deliberate.

"On the ridge," McQuiston said. "Two hundred yards?"

"Two hundred, three hundred . . ." Calistro's expression was a shrug. He looked up at the bending grass tops, listening to the sounds of the shooting.

"They must not have seen us duck out," McQuiston said. "That's hard to believe."

Calistro opened the action of his rifle and thrust the stock away from him to see if he had jammed the barrel with mud when he dived out of the yard. The barrel was clear. He said, "On the right that one does not care about the cost of bullets."

McQuiston heard lead whine off a rock at the cabin. They would not be wasting bullets on the fireplace, so they must be shooting close to the foundation, guessing that he and Calistro were lying inside on the floor.

Calistro moved the grass carefully. With his finger he drew in the air a wide figure like the horns of a steer.

"There are low places where we can creep to the hill."

"Yeah." McQuiston grinned. "If there ain't over a dozen, the two of us can surround them." He spoke in English and his levity was lost on Calistro. "There's sure to be three men, maybe more. Let's try it."

Calistro was already wriggling up the meadow. McQuiston bellied around and went the other way. He made two approaches toward the hill after a long crawl. Both times the grass began to run too thin for cover and he had to back up.

On his third effort he found a dip that angled toward the ridge. It was not deep but it was enough to cover a man who was willing to grind his belt buckle in an Indian creep.

He gained the edge of the timber and lay down behind a stump, listening to position the rifleman he was flanking. The man was spacing his shots evenly and the trees ahead diffused the sounds, but the direction was clear enough.

McQuiston began the last phase of his stalk.

The sniper Calistro was trying to flank farther up the ridge slowed down his rate of fire, but suddenly he went into a spurt. He might have seen Calistro, but McQuiston doubted it. A man long used to fighting Apaches, Calistro could move like one.

After a time the more distant firing steadied into a more even effort, and then McQuiston realized what had happened. The sounds were different, coming from a lighter rifle. There were at least two men on Calistro's side of the affair.

For a while McQuiston lay in a blowout of quartz

rocks. He was much closer to his man now. Below him was a small gulch that drained down to the camp Calistro had made. Beyond the gulch the trees stood close together, making a solid clump of green. The man was on the far side of the trees, or at least quite close to the far side.

McQuiston began to creep down between the rocks. He took his time. As long as the firing was directed at the cabin, he and Calistro were ahead of the game.

Avery Teague had been relieved once by Van Buskirk, which had made the change in the firing that McQuiston had heard. Now Teague, after a time with the horses, returned to resume his original post.

Van Buskirk looked over his shoulder. "You didn't stay any ten minutes, Teague."

"It was nearer twenty. Go on back to the horses."

"Are they all right?"

"Sure, but Squanto said—"

"Let *him* go back then." There wasn't much to this shooting, with the men inside the cabin offering nothing in return, but it was better, Van Buskirk thought, than watching horses which were no longer nervous over the sound of shots. Just for the hell of it he put a bullet through the smoke pipe and watched soot darken the thin stream of gray smoke.

"It's your turn," Teague said. "Go on. I ain't going clear over there after Squanto."

"The horses will be all right." Van Buskirk aimed at the third log of the cabin and then lowered his rifle without firing. "They must be in there. How could they have got out? Did you and Squanto—"

"I watched the place all the time after I left Squanto. Nobody came out. Their horses are there, ain't they? And we saw one man go in."

"That was before we came on down here," Van Buskirk said. "If they're in there why don't they do something?"

"The only place they can shoot back from is the window. I've been dropping one in there every now and then." Teague walked forward and settled down beside Van Buskirk.

"I still say there's something wrong." Van Buskirk withheld fire. "If I was down there, I'd have some of the chinking knocked out, or else I'd be laying near the front corner, outside, making it hot up here."

"The logs are hewed to set tight against each other," Teague said. "You don't notice things, Billy. And I can kill any man who tries to make it hot up here by shooting from around the front corner." Teague splashed a shot into the dirt at the corner of the cabin. "Like that, see."

Van Buskirk stared into the woods on his left. "I still say something's gone haywire."

Sprawled between two rocks near a dense stand of pines, Squanto was sure that something was wrong below. He had seen too much of war to believe that men like McQuiston and Calistro would lie in the cabin without firing a shot in return. It was possible of course. He had no intentions of finding out the truth the hard way. But he had been taken in painfully so many times by Confederate infantry commanders . . .

He held his fire for a long time.

Van Buskirk was not shooting either. Then Squanto heard Teague's rifle rip the silence. Minutes afterward, Van Buskirk fired. Then Teague once more. A short time later the lighter sound of Van Buskirk's rifle came again. Squanto sighed. After one spell apiece with the horses, the two of them over there had decided to stay together. Squanto rose. It was time for a conference anyway.

The crack of a pistol shot in the timber and a series of high yells made him kneel quickly. He heard the thump of running horses and another pistol shot. Deliberately he faced off to his right. There was no hurry now. Someone had got to the horses while Teague and Van Buskirk were having an afternoon social.

Squanto started around the stand of pines. It was like old times, when you thought you had the Rebs in front of you and then they came slashing against your flank, or screaming down on reserve companies in the rear. To hell with the horses. See what kind of strength was on the right.

McQuiston was crouching in the rocks when Squanto saw him. McQuiston's rifle was ready and Squanto's was not. Squanto reacted instantly to the situation, lunging sidewise to cover a fraction ahead of the shot he could not have matched. The tree that had been behind him an instant before received the bullet.

And now the pine that Squanto stood behind was not big enough to shield him. He dropped to his hands and knees and scrambled away to better cover. Shredded wood jumped from the side of the tree as Squanto went down. With a screen between him and McQuiston,

Squanto looked back calmly at the gashed trunk. McQuiston was serious as hell; you couldn't blame him.

Unhurriedly Squanto backed away, keeping the clump of trees between him and McQuiston. The silence behind him said that Teague and Van Buskirk didn't know where Calistro was. Squanto reviewed the situation as if it were a skirmish of major proportions.

The attacking force had been flanked on one wing and surprised in the rear. Van Buskirk was stout enough but he was wild and unpredictable. When the heat was up in him, Teague would fight anything, but he was no man to play Indian games with Calistro; with two men against him, Calistro would be operating like a Ute.

Van Buskirk leaped up with a guilty expression when the first shot came from the direction of the horses. He started on the run and then he came to his senses and slowed down, circling in carefully to where the horses had been. Their tracks pointed straight down the hill.

Van Buskirk accepted the blame and went after them.

The silence soon became a tremendous pressure on Teague. He kept looking from right to left, then twisting to see behind him. The cabin below mocked him.

Two shots sounded on his right. Neither was from Squanto's rifle. Then the silence again. There was more gloom among these tall trees than Teague had noticed before. Van Buskirk was gone, no telling where. Someone had shot twice over where Squanto was and Squanto's rifle had not answered.

Time went in great leaps for Teague. There came to him a sensation of loneness, a feeling that all support was gone, the creeping fear that can rout a company, a battalion. He got up and went away swiftly, trying to look all around him as he walked. It was not cowardice that chased him, but a threat built from the silence, and the knowledge that he had lost all contact with his companions.

He was going quietly among the trees when he saw the man on his left, moving in the same direction. Teague put his rifle up and almost fired before he recognized Squanto. An instant later Squanto saw him and pointed down the hill, in the direction where the horses had been.

They went together past the place where they had left the horses. Following the tracks, they came from the timber and saw Van Buskirk far away on a bare hillside. He was riding Squanto's horse. He went over the hill and out of sight.

"There's a man for you!" Teague said bitterly.

"He'll be back when he catches the other two." Squanto wrinkled his nose. He walked over to the mouth of a small gulch and looked down on the swollen body of a dun horse. "What happened to that, I wonder? Why, hell, that's the packhorse they had that day at June's."

His calmness irritated Teague, who kept watching the timber behind them. "Let's get out on the other side of that little hill there."

They got behind an isolated knob, putting it between them and the timber. By looking between the rocks they could see behind them, but Squanto didn't bother to turn his head. Teague was taking care of that operation well enough.

It was a half hour before they saw Van Buskirk again. He came into the open on the bare hillside, leading two horses. Squanto raised his rifle and Van Buskirk came toward them, straight across open country.

"That's a fool thing to do!" Teague cried. "They can pick off the horses!"

"They won't. I'll bet on that."

No shots came from the timber. Van Buskirk brought the horses up, his face showing anger against himself. Give him a little seasoning and he'd be a good man to ride with anywhere, Squanto thought.

Teague's hot temper lashed out at Van Buskirk. "Well, you bollixed things again!"

"You both did," Squanto said, without any heat. "Now let's all keep our mouths shut and go home."

He was the only one who showed no uneasiness while his back was still within rifle range of the timber. When they were down in the sage hills once more, he began to laugh. "Lost our horses and ran like militia!" he boomed. "That's what I call a good afternoon's work!"

Van Buskirk started to grin, but when he saw Teague's dark expression he looked away and held his face straight.

On the Tumbling road they met Tom Hosmer, who was taking a mare to stud at Copperwhaite's ranch. He had seen them come from the draw that led to Buffalo Meadows. He made a quick guess about their business, and then he veiled his thoughts behind a squint that wrinkled his whole face. Common sense told him to greet the three men carelessly and ride on, but he had news that was hard to keep and a twisting curiosity about its effect.

Hosmer could not keep still. "They found Corbett."

"The devil they did," Squanto said. "Who?"

"Those two up at Buffalo Meadows." The park was not a safe subject, so Hosmer tried to slide away quickly from it. "He was in the barn at the Y until this morning. Charlie Nye took a look at him and then he had Troy bury him."

Hosmer did not like the silence.

After a time Van Buskirk asked, "What did Nye say?"

"Nothing. You know Charlie." The attitude of his three listeners increased Hosmer's unease. He wished he had kept still. He could not. "Nye was up this way this morning. He was looking—Well, he's back at the Y again, I hear."

"What are you trying to say?" Van Buskirk asked.

"Nothing. I just—"

"You said he was looking." Teague's meanness ran in his voice. "Looking for what, Hosmer?"

"I don't know!"

"You meant he was looking for us," Teague said. "What are you trying to make of it?"

"Nothing, nothing, Avery! All I said was he came up the river. What for, I don't know."

"You think you do," Teague said. "Why don't you accuse us of killing Corbett?"

"I ain't hinting at nothing," Hosmer muttered. He jerked the tow rope on the mare and rode away.

"So they found Corbett," Squanto mused. "I've always wondered what happened to him."

"Who hasn't?" Teague said. "Who hasn't?"

It was too late for Van Buskirk to get in an oblique denial as the other two had done, without his words sounding strained and hollow, so he said nothing but he cursed them both for hinting that he was guilty of Corbett's death.

CHAPTER 12

The slender man who came riding down the park seemed well fitted to his wiry grulla. McQuiston did not recognize the rider until he was quite close. He spoke softly to Calistro then, "Nye, the deputy sheriff from Columbine."

"So?" An expression of dislike came instantly to Calistro's features.

Charlie Nye's mild brown eyes roved over the shattered window in the west wall of the cabin. He looked at the scarred logs and the ragged tear in the stove pipe. It was a quick, thorough survey. He said casually, "Made any deals for cows yet?"

"Not yet," McQuiston said, "but we figure to."

"Angus Copperwhaite would be your best bet. He's a good man to do business with—after you beat his price down."

"Thanks," McQuiston said. "Have a bite with us?"

When Nye started to wash at the bench near the door he gave no indication that he had seen Calistro deliberately dump the water pail a few minutes before. Whistling cheerfully, Nye went to the spring with the pail. He was washing when McQuiston said to Calistro in Spanish, "That was a poor deed, Ben. Why did you do it?"

"Let all *rurales* work a little for their food," Calistro said swiftly in his native language.

Nye dried his face and ran his hand over his sparse sandy hair. He lifted the water pail. "Do you wish this to be dumped again, Calistro?" His Spanish was very good. "No? Then I will leave it."

There were small shards of glass still caught in the rough places of the floor and fat, bright splinter scars on the walls where bullets had carried through at the joining of the logs. Nye looked curiously at the east window, which Squanto had not touched with a bullet.

In the middle of the meal the deputy said, "Calistro, the man you found was Len Corbett, sure enough. There were two or three things in his pockets that cinched it. I had him buried on the hill near the Y this morning."

"And so?" Calistro asked.

Nye took a swallow of coffee. "You know how to make that, McQuiston. I've been drinking restaurant slop longer than any man should have to." After a time he answered Calistro's question. "Why, I guess that's about all there is to it. One rib was busted up, maybe from a bullet, maybe from a fall. Miss Darland tells me you found him in the rocks. I'd like to see the place."

"I will take you there," Calistro said.

"Just tell me and I can find it."

After eating, Nye examined the pistol McQuiston had picked up. The deputy hung it back on a nail on the wall after a brief inspection. "I'll take it along, of course. I don't know why, though."

He went on foot to find the place Calistro had told him about. Going through the trees on the ridge behind the cabin, he saw the glint of a rifle case on the ground and went over to it. There was a litter of them on the brown needles. He poked around until he determined that the cases had come from two rifles. He put one of each caliber into his pocket.

Instead of going then to where Calistro had directed him, he spent an hour on the ridge, walking about slowly, reading the story of what had happened. He grinned when he saw where the horses had been spooked.

In the rocks where Corbett had been found there was no story to read, except that a rider would have had to get his horse where a horse could not go in order to fall off it and land where Corbett had landed.

For a while Nye stood in the hollow of the rocks, staring at the ground, thinking of the indrawn, defensive attitude of Troy Clinton when he had tried to talk to the old man about Corbett, and other matters. Nye knew his own persuasive powers, but he had failed completely with Clinton.

After finding that Squanto, Teague and Van Buskirk were all away from their ranches, Nye had spent the afternoon with Clinton, helping him with chores. He had played pitch with him that night in the bunkhouse at the Y, and all of it had not loosened Clinton one bit. Nye was not sure even now whether Clinton knew anything worth telling or whether he was constitutionally a tight-mouth.

There was a rumor that Squanto Whitcomb had got

Clinton to talk once when they were on a drunk together in Columbine about a month after the Los Pinos hanging, and that old Troy had told Squanto a great many facts not commonly known. Nye had his doubts, although he did not discount the story entirely.

He went back to the cabin.

"Find anything of interest?" McQuiston asked.

"About Corbett? No." Nye gave Calistro a casual glance. "What happened to the little dun somebody dragged down to the mouth of the gulch back there?"

"It died," Calistro said solemnly.

"It looked dead, all right." Nye's face was grave.

"Old age, a bad stomach, the liver—something," Calistro said. "A fine horse too."

"Oh yes." Nye smiled faintly. The shells in his pocket clinked against each other as he went down to the corral to saddle up.

McQuiston grinned at Calistro. "You didn't win much off him, did you?"

When Nye was ready to go, McQuiston gave him the pistol. "Oh, that," the deputy said absently, shoving the weapon under his belt. He eyed the bullet marks in the cabin logs with a quizzical expression. "Thanks for the grub, boys." He swung into the saddle, a trim, mild-mannered man who still did not look like he belonged in the hills above the Tumbling.

The corners of his mouth lifted slightly as he studied McQuiston and Calistro, and then Nye rode away at a brisk trot.

Calistro watched him with a musing look. "He will go

now to talk to our friends of yesterday, if he has not seen them already. I think he would talk to the devil, if there was a reason. His horse is good. He treats it well. He did not ask questions to make the ears deaf, but he saw everything.

"One might say he is a man to like, but of course it is very difficult for one to love those who are of the law, is it not the truth?"

"We have found it so sometimes, yes," McQuiston said. "When shall we get the horse Van Buskirk owes us?"

"It is better to send a message to him, telling him to bring the horse here to us, which he will not do."

"And let him sweat awhile?" McQuiston said.

"Yes. Then we will go to him and get our horse." Cruelty lay like a pale light on Calistro's somber features.

"In the meantime, how about the cows?"

"Buy them," Calistro said. "We have gold. Madero gold."

"It was honest, Ben."

"All gold is dishonest after it rises from the earth and passes through the hands of men. But buy the cows." Calistro smiled. "And with them, a bull."

CHAPTER 13

On his way to the Copperwhaite place the next morning McQuiston met Tom Hosmer leading a sorrel mare. He did not know the man but Hosmer guessed who McQuiston was and introduced himself.

"How's things up your way?" Hosmer asked. "No

trouble, I hope." He tried to be off-hand, but McQuiston sensed the furious curiosity behind the man's squint. Here was a gossip, a man to spread a tale, and he was just what McQuiston wanted.

"Very peaceful around the meadows," McQuiston said. "We get sort of lonely."

"Yeah." Hosmer was disappointed.

"We did have a little trouble a while back. Someone came into our camp and put a rope on a horse that wasn't used to a rope." McQuiston shook his head. "It cost us the horse."

"Too bad."

"Yes, it was," McQuiston said mildly. "Do you ever happen to run into Van Buskirk?"

Hosmer's interest picked up. "Sometimes."

"When you see him, if you will, tell him we'd like him to bring up another horse to replace the one we lost. Would you do that?"

"Sure. I don't know when I'll see him, but I'll tell him when I do." Hosmer was in a hurry to be off.

Van Buskirk would get the message today; McQuiston was sure of that. He went down the road humming. On the way back, if things worked out, he'd stop to see June.

Angus Copperwhaite was drenching a horse with laudanum when McQuiston arrived at the ranch. Dan was holding the rope which ran through an eyebolt in a barn rafter, keeping the animal's head up. Old Angus gave McQuiston a sharp nod and went on with his task of pouring the fluid from a long-necked bottle down the throat of the sidling horse.

When the last drop was gone, Angus motioned to his son to take the horse away. He put the bottle on a shelf beside a large medicine chest and turned to McQuiston with an expression of reserve. "Well?"

"I thought I might buy a few head of cows, if you've got any for sale, Mr. Copperwhaite."

"I heard you were staying."

They talked it over while leaning against the poles of a corral. The ranch buildings sprawled for a hundred yards along the base of a hill. The meadows were the widest of any on the Tumbling, and from the north the Elkhorn wound its way through another rich hayland bottom to join the larger river just below the ranch. The whole place had an air of prosperity and friendliness, but Angus was still withholding judgment on McQuiston.

McQuiston started to wave at Evaleth when she came out on the porch. He caught himself, wondering if Angus had observed the half completed gesture.

"Cattle are going up this fall," Angus said.

"Or down. We talked some of waiting to see."

"You can't hold cattle on Buffalo Meadows in an average hard winter, McQuiston, unless you intend to cut hay and build sheds."

"We'll try it for one winter. After that we hope to get land in the valley."

Angus watched McQuiston thoughtfully. "You'll have to go out on the range with me a day or two. I haven't got anything here to sell."

McQuiston watched Evaleth go back inside. "All right."

He spent three days on the Copperwhaite range, and

was impressed by old Angus' cattle sense and the respect his riders showed the Scot. He decided to buy thirty head of cows, with their calves, and one good shorthorn bull. On the way back to the ranch he parried all morning with Angus before they agreed on the price.

When that was done, Copperwhaite's red face cracked with a big grin. "If you're a horse breaker, I can make another small deal with you."

"I'm just ordinary at that. My partner, though, is the best there is."

"Send him down," Angus said.

They reached the ranch at sundown. Mrs. Copperwhaite called from the porch that they could have supper in fifteen minutes. After they put their horses away, Angus opened the medicine chest in the barn. It held more whiskey than medicine. He blew hay dust from two glasses and poured them full.

They were having a second nip when Angus said suddenly, "My daughter was at the Darland place the night you fought Squanto, wasn't she?"

McQuiston didn't know what to say.

"I see she was." Angus nodded. "It's a funny thing, McQuiston—" He finished his drink. "You're Irish?" When McQuiston nodded, Angus went on. "I know she goes there and I don't like it, but as long as her mother and her think I don't know, I let it go. That is, as long as her brothers are along.

"It's like my whiskey here. My wife hates it. She wouldn't have it in the house if it would save someone of dying from colic. So I'm obliged to do my drinking in the barn. She knows it, and says nothing." Angus poured another round. "That's the way of marriage, McQuiston. You compromise on a lot of things, unless your head's so hard you're determined to have it busted. If you ever get married, remember what I've said."

"I will." McQuiston realized that Angus had accepted him. Besides looking over cattle, the Scot had been looking over McQuiston; and they had spent one day more on the range than was necessary. Now Angus was giving time-worn advice about marriage. McQuiston was amused. The old boy always had a plan in the back of his mind.

"Are you much of a drinking man, McQuiston?"

"I've had my share, I guess."

Angus put the bottle away. "Have you heard the story that June Darland served Roby a foul trick?"

"No." After a few moments of waiting it came to McQuiston that Angus was not going to gossip. He had asked a question and that was all.

"I don't say there's truth in it or not. You'll hear the tale some day. You judge for yourself. Let's go eat."

There was a solid, comfortable atmosphere in the Copperwhaite home that impressed McQuiston and made him feel the loneliness of his own life. He guessed it was the strong family spirit of the group. Nobody was the absolute boss of the household.

There were two younger brothers here tonight that McQuiston had not seen before. He found out that an older daughter had married and moved away the summer before, and that there was another son having a fling at mining in the San Juan. Angus' wife was a strong-featured woman whose face mirrored the suns and winters of the Tumbling country.

But the trials had weathered her only, McQuiston decided, instead of wearing her down. Like old Angus during the three days on the range, Mrs. Copperwhaite was sizing McQuiston up quite thoroughly. Something in her voice kept troubling him, until at last he recognized what it was. She was Irish, a generation or so removed from the crossing of the water, perhaps.

This family then was of the hardy stock that had pushed into the dark forests west of the Colonies, gray- and blue-eyed men and women looking on the tossing trees, driving on and on across the great prairies, dying, living, grim faces behind long rifles, laughter in lonely cabins . . . No wonder they acted like a family, McQuiston thought. Their heritage was a strong steel cable of struggle, of hardship, and of winning together.

Evaleth reached past McQuiston's shoulder to pour him coffee. He turned his head to look at her and she caught the odor on his breath. Her eyes crinkled and she said under her breath, "Whew!" McQuiston grinned, and then he saw Mrs. Copperwhaite watching him.

"I'll deliver the cows," Angus said.

"If you can't spare the men, just tell me where Calistro and I can pick the herd up." The drive to Buffalo Meadows had been worrying McQuiston. He knew what could happen on the way.

"I'll deliver the cows. I've made up my mind."

Dan said, "Good! It's time somebody in this country declared himself against what's been happening at Buffalo Meadows."

"Is that so, Daniel?" Angus asked. "I'll put you on

point when we start. We'll see what happens if Squanto Whitcomb comes along and decides to lift you out of the saddle with one finger and spank you."

McQuiston stayed in the bunkhouse with the two older boys. Mark still had no use for him, watching him with blank sullenness or with studied resentment. When Dan suggested a card game, Mark shook his head. He walked out.

Dan laughed. "He's nuts about June Darland, and he thinks you've jumped ahead of everybody since you came. He'll get over it. That's the way it is with kids his age."

"Oh?" McQuiston held a straight face. Dan was nineteen, two years older than Mark.

"I was sort of crazy about her once myself," Dan said. "She laughed at me, I'll admit, but that wasn't the reason I gave up."

"No?"

"Naw. It don't work out with June, somehow. I don't know what it is. She's pretty and she's full of life, but there's times when she seems to me like she's twice as old as I am. After a little of that you just shy away."

"You don't mean you sort of get run away, do you?"

"Teague and that bunch? Huh-uh! They try to cripple outsiders that show interest in June, like they jumped you, McQuiston, but it wasn't them that scared me away from June. It was June herself that made me leery. I'll tell you something about women—"

"Some other time," McQuiston said. "Right now I'd rather know how you think cattle will make out in the park during the winter."

134

McQuiston left before sunrise the next morning. Evaleth came out in the yard to tell him good-bye. The vigor of her, the bubbling life and brightness, were as apparent at the start of the day as any other time. McQuiston liked the woman; he liked the whole family, for that matter.

He rode away, anxious to get to the Y, and he was thinking of what June had told him of running to meet the sun when she was a girl.

Angus and his wife watched through the window. Their daughter stopped on the porch and turned to watch McQuiston as he rode away.

"Now it could be that there is the man for her," Angus said. "I'll not say I'm sure, but—"

"Let *her* find out, if you please."

"Indeed I will. I was never one to tell others what to do, except when they needed to be told. Now if McQuiston begins to come here to call on her—"

"Marriages are not made by fathers, Angus, and not in heaven either," Mrs. Copperwhaite said. "Because the man will pay cash for thirty cows is no reason—"

"This is no matter of business! I—"

"Then don't try to make it one. In time Evaleth will be married, and you or I will have very little to do with it." Mrs. Copperwhaite began to pick up dishes as noisily as a woman could.

Angus went outside. He hesitated on the porch, of a mind to make some casual inquiry to determine what his daughter thought of McQuiston. Sound judgment told him that Evaleth would see through him like a pane of

135

glass. He went away to see about the horse with colic. No woman could give him any advice about that, at least.

Evaleth came inside to help her mother. They went through their work routine swiftly and without comment until Mrs. Copperwhaite said, "Once you're married, you'll find this work goes on forever."

"Who said anything about my getting married?"

"No one. I merely mentioned—"

"If you and Pa are thinking to palm off that McQuiston fellow on me, why you—"

"Perish the thought!" Mrs. Copperwhaite said. "What gave you that idea?"

"His head is full of June Darland."

"A good many men have had their heads turned by that lass, Evaleth."

"I don't want to talk about it!"

"Let's not then." Mrs. Copperwhaite looked at the strong, golden-colored arms dipping in and out of the copper sink, remembering with a sigh when her own flesh had been firm and tightly skinned; and when she had been so mad at Angus, a big red-cheeked lout of a boy, that she had sworn never to mention his name again. The years flew like eagles, but nothing ever changed greatly in the feelings of human beings.

Mrs. Copperwhaite said, "Your father has business in town at the end of the week, Evaleth. If Dan and Mark wish to take you to—"

"I'm not going back to the Y."

Evaleth's words ran swift and hard. The tone of anger was not there, but rather, a dark edge of fear, as if some

136

remembered horror lay in her mind.

"Was it the fight?" Mrs. Copperwhaite asked gently.

"No! I've seen men try to kill each other before."

"Well, then—"

"There's talk of a dance in two weeks at the school-house," Evaleth said. "Tom Hosmer mentioned it. I may go there."

"That's good." Watching her daughter narrowly, Mrs. Copperwhaite did not forget that a question had not been answered. Evaleth was no flighty girl, given to the megrims. Something at the Darland place had troubled her greatly; but her brothers had been along, close to her all the time . . . Still, it would not hurt to question them closely.

CHAPTER 14

Each time McQuiston saw June he was impressed anew with the striking clearness of her face, the shadow of sadness that seemed to hover in the background of her appearance, and the innocence that was like a rebuke. It was that way when he rode into her yard on his return from the Copperwhaite place.

Grandma Varnum was not there, and Clinton was gone somewhere, so McQuiston did not go inside. He told her about the cows he had arranged to buy.

"That's fine. It means you're going to stay." The orange-brown eyes smiled. "Didn't you have some trouble the other day?"

"Who said so?"

"Tom Hosmer. He was guessing, but he usually

knows what's going on."

"We had some trouble," McQuiston said.

"Was anyone hurt?" June moistened her lips.

"Nothing but the stove pipe." McQuiston grinned. "Will there be another dance here Saturday?"

June did not hear the question at once. She was studying McQuiston quietly. He asked again.

She shook her head. "Not after the way the last one turned out. Hosmer said there might be a dance at the schoolhouse week after next, though."

"Let's go."

"I haven't been to one of those for a year, Dallas."

"Then it's time you went. It's time the miserable people around this country—"

"No, no, don't say that. I'll go with you, but it may not be pleasant for either of us."

When he was out in the road, McQuiston could not remember the details of June's face. He felt a strong urge to go back, to look at her again, so that he could carry away the impression she made on him when he was close to her. There seemed to be no mystery when he was with her. She aroused his male instincts, she created sympathy without asking for it, and she made him hate Teague and the others who came to see her.

The faces of some women whose names were long forgotten were still clear in his memory, their smiles, the twisting of anger, the beckoning of love; but minutes after seeing June, McQuiston could not make her stand sharply outlined in his mind. Yet, he could not forget her, or even thrust her completely from his thinking for very long.

He was thinking of her when he met Billy Van Buskirk. He knew at once that Hosmer had given Van Buskirk the message about the horse. The two men stopped, facing each other in the road, with the dust of Van Buskirk's coming catching up to make a thin film between them.

McQuiston's voice was conversational. "When you brought the horses back to Squanto and Teague the other day, Calistro and me had you in our sights for a good hundred yards."

"Why didn't you shoot, McQuiston? You'll probably never get another chance like that."

McQuiston smiled pleasantly. He knew Van Buskirk expected to hear about the packhorse, and so McQuiston did not speak of it.

"Anything else on your mind?" Van Buskirk asked.

"Nothing much, except sometime this week we'll be driving a herd from the valley to the meadows. We'll follow the road all the way." McQuiston saw caution temper Van Buskirk's natural recklessness. Without giving the man a chance to answer, McQuiston rode away.

From a rocky point in the aspens Squanto and Van Buskirk looked down on the small herd crawling through the dust at the foot of Squire's Hill. Van Buskirk said, "No wonder McQuiston bragged that he'd come up the road."

There were seven riders with the herd.

Squanto sprawled against the rocks in silence. The Copperwhaites were down there, and they had brought two riders. Old Angus had declared himself; and that, more than the fact that cows would at last go into Buffalo Meadows, was the handwriting on the wall. Van Buskirk might be made to see it. Teague never would.

Squanto mulled it over. Anything within reason, he was willing to get for June, but now the price of Buffalo Meadows was too costly. She would have to change her mind about the park.

"What do you think?" Van Buskirk asked, with his eyes on the men below.

"I think you'd better take a horse to McQuiston and Calistro—before they come after it."

Van Buskirk's clothes rasped the stones as he scrabbled around to face Squanto. "You crazy?"

"I know when to back up, Billy."

"You'd let the meadows go! What about the bet?"

"Unless you want to go to murder, the meadows are lost," Squanto said. "The bet was a childish thing."

"The hell you say!"

"Charlie Nye is no idiot. He knows we hung Roby. He knows one of us killed Corbett." Squanto looked down the hill. "Angus and everyone else in the country knows it too. Buffalo Meadows just ain't worth the price, Billy. Maybe it never was." He paused. "Did you kill Corbett?"

"No!" Van Buskirk's anger flared up. "Did you?"

Squanto shook his head slowly. He grinned and knew at once it was a mistake. A fear and a terrible distrust showed in Van Buskirk's expression. "No, it wasn't me, Billy." But it was too late. Squanto knew he had lost a friend, his only friend in the whole Tumbling country since the hanging of Max Roby.

The herd was starting up Squire's Hill.

Squanto said, "Let's go back to Teague."

"I take it then that you're giving up the meadows without a fight?"

"We never owned an inch of the park, Billy."

"You're giving up June too?" Van Buskirk asked.

"No, but she's giving up the park, as far as I'm concerned. I'll make her understand."

"The hell you will!" Van Buskirk said. "She talks about wanting those meadows more than—"

"I know. She ran toward the sun when she was a little girl. She lay in the grass looking at the blue, blue sky. She wasn't no little girl when she lived there, Billy, and her story is to take in suckers like you and Teague." Squanto leaped off the rock and started away.

"Wait a minute!" Van Buskirk cried.

Squanto went on.

Van Buskirk clutched the butt grips of his pistol. He stared at the broad back. After a moment he let out his breath with a gusty sigh that gave him no relief inside. He jumped down and followed Squanto.

On the way back to Teague, Van Buskirk asked, "Who fired that shot on Los Pinos?"

Squanto gave him a quick look. "My God, Billy, you *are* behind, ain't you?" He studied Van Buskirk as a father might study a child who had erred because of lack of instruction. "It wasn't me."

Van Buskirk's face was bitter with doubt.

Teague was sitting behind a log with his rifle across his knees, looking to where the road was a long gash in the aspens. "They're both coming, huh?"

"Yeah," Squanto said. "And along with 'em, three Copperwhaites and two of Angus' men."

Teague kept staring at the narrow passage in the trees. When he raised his head to look at Squanto his face was hard and quiet. "What's Angus trying to do to us?"

"That's easy to see," Squanto said. "What are *we* trying to do?"

"You talk like a fool." Teague looked through the aspens once more. "It's not going to make any difference. Once they get fairly strung out in that lane down there, we'll scatter 'em from hell to breakfast."

Squanto sat down beside Teague. "We could do that." It had been the plan when they thought only two men would be with the herd. "But they got enough riders to eat those cows, Teague. We can still scatter the herd, but they'll have it scoured out of the aspens in three hours and be on their way up the hill again. It ain't worth it."

"They won't be on their way so fast if we dump a few men out of their saddles," Teague said.

Squanto glanced at Van Buskirk. Van Buskirk was not learning anything. He was chewing his lip and peering down the hill, and it was doubtful that his mind was on the talk.

"Last we saw, Dan Copperwhaite was out in front," Squanto said mildly.

"A Copperwhaite is no better than anyone else, once he sets himself against us," Teague said.

Once more Squanto looked at Van Buskirk, and again Van Buskirk was too wrapped up in some dark thought of his own to see what was before his eyes.

142

"The park is lost," Squanto said. "Make your minds up to that."

Van Buskirk came alive then, grinding out his objections. A tight fury leaped in Teague, and both men slammed their arguments against Squanto. It was like the clanging of dull chisels on granite. In bitter, low-voiced anger Teague and Van Buskirk battered away, but they could not break the smallest chip from Squanto's conviction.

They wore out. Squanto stared at Van Buskirk. "You, Billy, have you lost your senses trying to get at Calistro?"

"We came here to break up that herd!" Van Buskirk's recklessness was speaking for him.

Squanto had hoped for something better, but now he was not going to waste more time in argument. He sat like a great lump, looking down the hill. The first rider came in sight, Dan Copperwhaite. He was riding high in the saddle, peering up the road as if he expected trouble.

The herd made the turn into the straight run through the aspens, a slowly heaving mass of animals that gave the appearance of being twice as large as it was. On the flanks the riders were crashing their horses through the trees. Squanto caught a glimpse of McQuiston.

"Let them get closer," Teague said. His rifle was resting across the log.

Van Buskirk was crouched beside him, his rifle slanting downhill. Calistro came into view, ducking his head under a limb.

Squanto drew his left arm across his chest, reaching up to scratch his shoulder. He looked sidewise at

Teague, and then he swung the bent arm in a driving motion that carried no more than a foot. His elbow struck Teague under the ear. The impact hurled Teague against Van Buskirk, and then Teague fell backward, unconscious on the damp leaf mold. His rifle slid down the log, pointing toward the sky.

Knocked over from his crouching position, Van Buskirk scrambled to his knees. For an instant he was confused. Squanto was sitting quietly. Teague was lying on his back, gray with shock, completely still.

"That's all I'm going to do for you, Billy," Squanto said. He rose quietly. "If you've got a lick of sense, which I used to think you had, you'll hit him again if he starts to come out of it before that herd is gone."

Van Buskirk pivoted around, with his rifle half raised. "I ought to drill you, Squanto!"

"Yeah, yeah," Squanto said. He moved a little farther into the trees so that he could not be seen from the road. "I ought to lecture you, too, but what's the use?"

"Teague and me are done with you for good!"

"Sure, Billy. The three of us were done with each other the day we hung Roby." The herd was passing within fifty yards, almost entirely hidden by the dense growth of aspens.

Squanto turned his back and walked away. For a half minute Van Buskirk stared uneasily at the place where he had gone. Teague lay like a dead man, with the toes of his boots turned out.

No sound of shots came to Squanto as he rode away. He went directly to the Y, harried for one of the few times in his life by the flow of time. He had always used time as an ally, while other men were prone to fight it; but now there was a nameless urgency sending him toward June.

She received him in the living room and said she was glad to see him. She was not particularly happy about seeing him, and Squanto knew the fact; but that was only one of the difficulties that he expected time to dissolve.

Squanto said, "How bad do you want Buffalo Meadows?"

June's eyes widened. "Why, I dream of being back there lots of the time. Sometimes I dream I'm a little girl again and—"

"You ain't a little girl, June, although you still act like it more than you should. The meadows are gone. You won't be going up there—ever."

"Gone?" she asked. "What do you mean?"

"I mean McQuiston and his partner have got the park for good," Squanto said. "And that suits me."

"You're afraid of them?"

Squanto watched June's eyes and the curling at the corners of her mouth. He did not even consider her question. "You don't care about the park, and you know it. I've been thick-headed not to understand that before. All the hell you've caused over that place. I know you sent Corbett up there. I'm guessing you sent McQuiston, and maybe you sent the Shepherd brothers too."

June's face was white. "You *know* I sent Corbett? What makes you think so?"

"Never mind. I came here to tell you you're not going

to have the meadows." He told her about the bet. He watched the way the knowledge pleased her. "And all the time we were fools enough to think you really wanted the park."

"Did you come here to insult me?"

"If the truth insults you, yes. I guess it does." A trace of humility came into Squanto's attitude. "I'm building the house you wanted, June. Will you come up and look at it?"

"Why?"

"It's for you."

The curl left June's lips and the clean, little-girl look returned. She walked close to Squanto, looking up into his face. "You never said anything about it before. You haven't asked me anything, Squanto. You know what I mean."

"I know what you mean, June."

"I don't want you to be hurt."

"I won't be."

June missed his meaning. "I just can't seem to make up my mind. You're all such good friends . . . Is it a big house, Squanto?"

"It'll do."

"But you've never asked me to marry you," June said.

"I'll get around to it."

June's lips thinned. "The others have asked already."

"I imagine." Squanto smiled. "I don't aim to be turned down when I ask."

"Don't you!"

She had made fools of Teague and Van Buskirk. There was no use for Squanto to tell her that, or to let her know how well he understood her. No human being, particularly a woman, wished to be completely understood. So Squanto made a small retreat. He said, "Well, I *hope* you'll agree to have me when I ask."

It was a heavy attempt at humbleness, a small gesture that lay without value across Squanto's tremendous confidence.

June was angered by it. "Get out!" she cried.

"Sure." Squanto went to the door. "If you say never come back, I'll do that too." He waited, knowing that his estimate of the woman was right: Not even anger could force her to make a break with any man who was attracted to her.

Squanto said, "Just tell me not to come back, and that's the way it will be." He gambled on his knowledge of June and his assurance seemed unbreakable, but all the time there was a deep fear in him that she would call the bluff. If she did do that, if she ever discovered the weakness in him, Squanto knew she would be lost to him.

He won. She understood his shrewd insight into her own nature. "I'll have McQuiston kill you!" she shouted.

Squanto shook his head. "He won't. You can't get by much longer with this working men against each other. You can't get by, either, with living alone here. There's a widow in Columbine, June, a fine, respectable woman. She's willing to come out here and—"

"Oh! So you've asked her already?"

"For your own good," Squanto said. "Look, June—"

"You're not running my life!"

"I'm trying to help you because—Well, I'm trying to help you."

"Get out, Uncle Squanto."

"That don't hurt me any more." Squanto grinned. But it did hurt, and worse than that, it stirred a rage that Squanto knew he could not afford. He held himself so that June did not know his feelings, for if she ever saw into him as he could see into her, she would have nothing but contempt for him.

He knew what she was and he loved her and he had to keep the knowledge of his love from her as long as he could.

He said, "You've made fools of men too long. There's got to be a change."

"Is that so, Uncle Squanto?"

"By God yes! You ruined your father's life. You've excited men to kill each other, but maybe you didn't realize what you were doing." Squanto paused. "You lied to us that day we came here asking about Roby, didn't you?"

In a curiously calm voice June asked, "What makes you think that?"

"I don't believe you ever told Roby you weren't going to marry him. You set us on him. You knew what would happen."

"Why don't you say it was because he'd made a will in my favor?" June was white-faced, calm, and her lips were curling at the corners.

"I wouldn't go that far, but I know you didn't tell us the truth that day."

"Go on, Uncle Squanto. Is there more?"

"Yes, by God, there is!" Squanto was disturbed because he could not control himself. "Teague was here right after your father left this place the day he was killed. Your father stopped at Rod Varnum's place for more than an hour. There was time—What did you tell Teague?"

"I suppose *you* would say I told him my father was trying to make me marry Max Roby. I suppose you'd say I made Teague so mad he went to Squire's Hill and—"

"No!" Squanto said. He had his anger under control. June's complete coldness frightened him, and he thought perhaps he had gone too far, making accusations that he could not believe himself. He was no better than the foul-mouthed gossips of the country. He shook his head violently. "I'm sorry, June."

She lowered her eyes. She looked pitiful and frail. "I'm sorry too, Squanto, that someone as close to me as you would repeat the filthy talk about me." She turned away slowly and went to the porch and there she hesitated, holding both hands to her face.

"June!"

When she turned, Squanto saw that she was crying. "You're right, Squanto, I don't want you to go away." She gave him a tremulous smile and ran into the house.

Squanto rode away slowly. He looked as solid and unperturbed as the hills around him, but worries that he had never known before kept gnawing at him. Now that he was no longer looking at June, facts that Troy Clinton had told him came back strongly and to them he added guesses. The blackness of Los Pinos crept out and mocked him.

He knew that from the day he first wanted June Darland a net of complications had started to grow around his life and now the net was very strong. He knew too much about June and still he loved her.

Suppose McQuiston, too, was willing to overlook the things in her that would turn a weaker man away? If it came to that, then Squanto would have to kill McQuiston.

It was a miserable thought, for Squanto was not inherently a violent man; but he had traveled so far in a hard, straight line of desire that deflecting him now would be like trying to turn the course of a mighty rock crashing down a mountainside.

CHAPTER 15

On the way to the schoolhouse dance June was eager and talkative. Her attitude doubled McQuiston's anxiety, for sober reflection had told him the whole idea was wrong. Now June was so happy he could not turn back.

From the time they went inside the mistake was apparent. If a delegation had met them at the door and forbidden them entrance, it would have been easier to bear than the polite cruelty of the whole affair.

The women ignored June. Mark and Dan Copperwhaite asked her to dance, and a few other young bucks came around hesitantly. The married men were gravely polite, but they drifted away from every conversation with McQuiston when June was with him.

Evaleth spoke to June, but her greeting was swift, and then a reserved expression tightened Evaleth's features and she hurried away.

McQuiston found no open source of hostility to challenge. It became an evening of maddening frustration. June took it with a set smile. Her face was strained and pale but she showed, McQuiston thought, high courage.

In the middle of a dance she said, "Don't you think we've had enough, Dallas?"

"No! We'll stay till the last dog is hung. That is, unless you want to leave."

"I'll stay if you wish. I'm used to this sort of treatment." June's voice was low. She smiled at McQuiston.

"Where's Grandma Varnum?"

"The Varnums went into town this morning, so they could all be there for church tomorrow."

"It'd be a little different if she was here." McQuiston stared around the room. He heard the music and laughter—and he and June were alone in the midst of it. Only a group of older married women taking care of sleepy children stared back at him with outright disapproval.

Angus Copperwhaite met his glance for a moment, and then turned to speak to a man beside him. When McQuiston took June back to an empty seat at the end of the dance, four women sitting in flanking chairs began to talk of the necessity of looking after the coffee in the kitchen. All four rose and left.

Mark Copperwhaite, stiffly ignoring McQuiston, came over to ask June for the next dance. McQuiston was grateful for the break. He went out the side door to cool his feelings in the night air. He was standing at the corner of the building when he heard the men talking.

". . . she did too! She rigged the whole deal up with Max Roby. She was going to marry him as soon as he signed over a chunk of his land to her old man and made a big, fat will—"

"You don't know no more than anyone else, Al. It was her old man that made the deal in the first place."

"The hell it was!" Al said. "My father says Fred Darland was as honest as they come. June's the one that got everything fixed up. Then somebody killed her old man and she seen a good chance to put Van Buskirk and them others on Roby's tail so she could collect on the will. She never was going to marry Roby. Of course she probably gave him a little just to—"

McQuiston went around the building on the run. He broke through a group standing beside a buggy and grabbed the speaker by the coat. With a short chop McQuiston slapped him back against the buggy wheel. He yanked the fellow forward and slapped him again.

The man tried to twist away. He ducked his head into light coming from one of the side windows and McQuiston saw that he was not a man, but a terrified boy. He let go of the youth's coat and looked around.

The whole group was composed of kids.

One of them, tall and awkward-looking in a too-tight coat, stammered defiance. "You got a lot of guts, McQuiston, jumping on Al."

Two boys ran toward the front door of the schoolhouse.

152

"Kid or not," McQuiston said to Al, "you've got a loose tongue." He turned away and started around the schoolhouse. Men hurrying toward the buggy bumped against him. Somebody ran past him, cursing him and June in the same breath.

Angus met him at the side door. "You'd best take her on home, McQuiston. I took you for a man with better sense." Scottish burrs growled on Angus' tongue as he spoke.

"I'll go when we're ready."

A dozen men stood behind Angus. One of them said, "There'll be no more dancing until you do go."

Around the building a heavy voice yelled, "Hit my kid! I don't care how tough he is, I'll break this single-tree over his head, the sonofabitch!"

There came the sound of a scuffle and another man said, "Take it easy, Bissell. He'll go."

June pushed her way through the men behind Angus. "I'm ready, Dallas."

"Good riddance!" a woman yelled.

Ashamed of himself and angry against circumstances, McQuiston drove June up the road in her buggy.

"It's all right," June said. "We weren't having much fun anyway. Who did you hit?"

"Some half grown kid named Al."

"Al Bissell. Did you knock him down?"

"No."

"Was he talking about me?"

"No."

"Yes he was, Dallas. Tell me what he said."

"He said you tricked Max Roby into thinking you

153

were going to marry him."

The buggy wheels ground through the night, and June was silent for a long time. "The old story. You don't believe it, do you?"

"No."

June sighed. She put her hand on McQuiston's shoulder. "Did you hurt Al?"

"I didn't hurt him any. Let's forget about it." The lights and music of the schoolhouse fell behind them. They were alone in the night, with the horse clopping along steadily. McQuiston said, "You can't stay alone much longer, June. Why don't you get married?"

"I've considered it. Who do you suggest I marry?"

The suggestion had been easy; the answer was something else. McQuiston tried to carry it off lightly. "There's plenty of men. Why, there's me, even."

He sensed that June was displeased with his light manner. She said nothing. McQuiston realized that if he tried to smooth things over, he would blunder in deeper. Marriage. It was a startling thought to a man who had wandered all his life.

Taking up with a woman was not as simple as taking up with land. The earth was made of land. If one place grew tiresome, you rode away between suns to find another place that suited you; but marriage was a binding settlement, a final move.

He considered the fact that no woman had ever attracted him like June. He wanted her, and she, too, had shown her interest in him; but it was not a simple matter to be settled on impulse.

McQuiston spoke carefully. "There's some things that

will have to be settled before I can ask any woman to marry me. The park, for one. Then, later on, I want to get land on the river."

June made no comment. McQuiston had a feeling that he had failed her.

The horse turned into the yard at the Y without any pressure down the lines. Clinton came from the bunkhouse, trudging along the lane of light from the doorway. His voice was thick when he told McQuiston he would take care of the horse and the odor of whiskey was on his breath.

McQuiston walked to the bottom step with June. She went up one step and turned. Her arms went around McQuiston's neck with violent pressure and her kiss was an explosion that caught him unprepared, flattening his lips and leaving a burning sensation afterward.

She ran to the top of the steps and waited. McQuiston stared through the dark toward the sound of her breath. Down near the barns, without benefit of lantern, old Troy was unharnessing, mumbling to the horse.

McQuiston put one foot on the first step. Then he backed away suddenly and called good-night and went across the yard to saddle his bay. He heard the door of the house close quietly, but no light showed inside by the time he was riding away.

A horse came from behind the bunkhouse and followed him out on the road. McQuiston put his hand on his pistol and swung around.

"Rest easy, McQuiston," a deep voice said. "All's quiet along the lines tonight."

Squanto Whitcomb came up out of the dark, looming monstrously large as he rode close to McQuiston. "If you don't mind, I'll go along as far as the turn-off with you."

They rode beside each other, McQuiston peering warily across the space between them; and then a feeling of confidence in Squanto came to him. Whatever kind of enemy Squanto was, he was not a man to strike from the darkness. But still McQuiston rode with his senses sharply edged.

"You didn't put any shots through the window on your side of the cabin," McQuiston said.

"Charlie Nye mentioned that too. Maybe I'm not a good rifle shot, McQuiston."

The saddles creaked and the horses scuffed along, placing their feet carefully in the dark.

"How was the dance?" Squanto asked.

"We left early."

"Sure. You didn't help things any by taking her, did you?"

"Is it your business, Squanto?"

"Yes."

It was a simple pronouncement, without heat. McQuiston wondered if Squanto had been outside the schoolhouse tonight, or merely waiting all the time with Clinton. He guessed it was the latter; and he knew that if he had gone inside the house, Squanto would have taken him apart. It would have been Squanto's own fight, not one taken from Teague, as the first one had been.

A cool respect for Squanto ran up and down

McQuiston's spine as he stared through the night at the big man.

"We once made a bet about Buffalo Meadows," Squanto said. "Teague and Billy and me. Now I'm out of it."

"What kind of bet?"

"That doesn't matter, McQuiston."

They went on without saying anything to each other until they were a short distance from the Buffalo Meadows road.

"Have trouble at the dance?" Squanto asked.

"Not much."

"Who insulted her?"

"No one—openly," McQuiston said.

"You left early."

"That was my fault."

"What happened?" Squanto asked.

He would find out by tomorrow or the next day. McQuiston gave him bare details.

"The Bissell kid was talking about her, huh? You mean that's the first time you'd heard the story about June and Roby?"

"Maybe not the first time," McQuiston said, "but a filthy lie sounds no better by being repeated."

"That's right. But there's reasons for telling lies and it's hard for a man to understand. Maybe you shouldn't try to understand. Maybe you've got enough when you know something is a lie—and the other person knows you know."

McQuiston was puzzled. He didn't know what Squanto was talking about.

They came to the Buffalo Meadows road.

"That story about June and Roby," Squanto said, "it happens to be true." Without pause he went on into the darkness at a slow walk.

CHAPTER 16

At twenty minutes of ten on a Sunday morning the Varnums joined the promenade to church in Columbine. The harness was oiled and rubbed, the yellow-striped wheels of the buggy were washed and polished, and the girls, in newly starched dresses, were sitting demurely with Grandma Varnum.

Rodney was a sincerely religious man, but he made no attempt to restrain a feeling of satisfaction and worldly pride when Franklin G. Lathrop, president of the Cattlemen's Bank, driving his family to church in a new leather-topped Studebaker behind two spanking blood bays, hailed the Varnums cordially.

Rodney smiled and patted his wife's hand. "We haven't done so bad in the last ten years, have we?"

Emma's nod was sober, but she was happy and Rodney knew it. In the back seat with the girls, Grandma Varnum rumbled cheerfully, "Don't let it go to your head, Rod."

At the corner of Cottonwood and Virginia, Rodney had to pull up while the stage from Gold Camp crashed by on its glory run to the Winchester House, throwing dust in the faces of a half dozen teamsters driving loads of mining supplies. One of them reached out with his blacksnake and exploded the snapper within inches of

158

the stage driver's head. His brother muleskinners shouted lusty, profane applause.

A bouncer threw two men out of the Valley Saloon as the Varnums turned the corner. The two men resumed their fight on the wooden walk, rolling under a hitch rail just as the buggy passed them. The children gaped. Grandma Varnum bent an experienced eye on the scene. Emma said, "Don't look at them, girls."

Things were better up the street, where the more sober business of the town was concentrated. Substantial merchants waved at Rodney as he moved along behind slow freight wagons.

The crowd that had watched the arrival of the stage had not yet dispersed. Rodney saw the reason: Three bedizened women waiting for their luggage to be unloaded. Two of them were young and good looking. The third was broad and formidable, standing half a head higher than the flunky who was receiving the luggage from the rack.

One of the girls said, "Look at the feathers, Grandma!"

"Never mind," Emma said.

Rodney cleared his throat and glanced around. His mother was staring intently at the three women on the walk. It would be best to get by as quickly as possible; even after the long years, you couldn't tell what might happen.

He tried to hurry, but a wagon loaded with whiskey barrels came out of an alley and bucked the current of traffic crosswise. One irate teamster refused to give way. His wagon and the one loaded with barrels bumped hubs with a crash. A barrel rolled into the street, frightening the buggy horse of a young man driving with a girl. The horse reared and tried to turn and bolt.

The drivers of the wagons that had struck each other got down to argue. Traffic was in a knot, with all the freighters stopped to shout encouragement to the two men yelling at each other.

A deep voice carried across the uproar. "Carrie! Carrie Moffatt!"

Emma Varnum looked around at her mother-in-law. "Why, that's you."

Rodney knew instantly where the call had come from: The big woman near the stage. Now her lips were clamped, she seemed to be regretting her act, and she was not looking toward the buggy.

"Do you know any of those women, Grandma?" Emma asked.

"No!" Rodney said. He knew his neck was getting red. He looked at the barrel that had caused all the trouble, listened to the shouting, profane teamsters, and it seemed that sin had trapped him before the eyes of the world. He turned and faced his mother. "You don't know those women, do you?"

She saw the shame in his expression; it shocked her. "Yes," she said, "I do. That's Billy Bostwick. I knew her very well thirty years ago." Grandma Varnum began to climb out of the buggy. From the ground she looked at her son quietly. "You can pick me up at the hotel after church." She gathered up her skirts and made her way between the wagons to the walk.

Rodney saw Billy Bostwick's face break into a great

gold-plated grin just before she and his mother threw their arms around each other. He was afraid to look at his wife.

The two shouting teamsters vented their feelings and ran short of steam. They began to laugh. Together they picked up the barrel and threw it back on the wagon.

The young man got his frightened horse under control. Traffic unsnarled and moved up the street. Grandma Varnum went into the Winchester House with a woman named Billy.

"You never told me," Emma said.

"It was none of your business."

"I think it was."

During services Rodney got a pain in his shoulders from sitting so straight and staring so fixedly at the pulpit. He picked up Grandma Varnum afterward at the hotel and it seemed to him that half the town knew and was laughing at him. The family made the long drive home with the children doing most of the talking.

Once the girls were in bed, Grandma Varnum braced herself aggressively for a quarrel.

Emma said nothing. Rodney was silent too, steeped in his own misery, sitting at the kitchen table with his hands smothering a cup of coffee that had grown cold.

"All right, let's have it!" Grandma Varnum said. "I'm not good enough for the likes of you two, is that it?"

"That isn't it at all." Emma looked to her husband for support. Rodney said nothing.

"You're thinking it, both of you!" Grandma Varnum said.

"No such thing," Emma said. Again she tried to get

help from her husband. "Rodney—"

"I suppose you'd like me to go before the whole congregation and beg forgiveness. To hell with that!"

"We're asking nothing, Mother," Emma said.

"Don't 'mother' me! I know how I'll be regarded around here from now on!" Grandma Varnum stamped off to her room.

"Go in there, Rodney," Emma said.

"I'm trying to think."

"You're feeling sorry for yourself, you mean."

Grandma Varnum did not take long. She came from her room dragging a small rawhide trunk. The sight of it reminded Rodney of the moves they had made on the Mississippi, when he was old enough to know about his mother.

He tried to argue then, but he had waited too long. No arguments were going to turn his mother now.

"Get the buggy ready," Emma said.

"I'll get it myself!" Grandma Varnum said. "I'm going down to live with June."

The girls woke up and came streaming into the room, crying when they found out their grandmother was leaving. Emma had her hands full trying to quiet them.

In the end, Grandma Varnum hoisted her trunk into the buggy after Rodney had hitched up the horse. The old woman drove away and Rodney winced, afraid that she was going to crash against a gate post in the dark.

He went inside. Emma was coldly angry with him. She said, "Well, Rodney, you weren't much help."

"I didn't know what to say."

"Your trouble is you're ashamed of her."

"How can I help but be!" Rodney cried. For a while self-pity kept him from understanding what lay behind Emma's challenging expression. But suddenly he said, "You mean you aren't ashamed of what—"

"No," Emma said, "I'm not. And you're the last person in the world who should be." The extension of her thought ran on as effectively as spoken words: All that a mother had done for her son, never trying to strangle with her love, never asking, or even expecting, gratitude.

Rodney's wife could have said it but she did not; she looked at her husband and let him say it to himself.

"You're not the least bit ashamed of her?" Rodney insisted. He kept staring when Emma shook her head. She was not a pretty woman and never had been. Their brief courtship had been a simple arrangement based on practical need and respect. But once again, as in other troubled moments, Rodney Varnum knew how lucky he had been.

"She got out of that buggy today because she was ashamed of *you,* Rodney, not of herself."

Rodney nodded. A guilt he had felt for years was lifting from him. The pity was he had carried it so long by hiding the truth from Emma. He could face the world now because his wife had made him face himself first. Emma Varnum, showing the weariness of the long ride today, marked by the hardships of ten uncertain years, had done for him in a short time what he had been unable to do for himself during twenty years.

Emma was beautiful. Rodney got up and took her into his arms and after a time he said, "I'll saddle—"

"No, not now. When she's ready to come home, we'll both go after her. It will take patience, and then more patience after she comes back."

"The Y is no place for her."

"She believes in June. The last thing we want to do is to try to change her mind by force."

Rodney paced across the room. "There's going to be a killing at that place one of these days. I can't understand how Mother believes—" He stopped suddenly and looked at Emma. "Do *you* believe that story about June and Roby?"

"Yes."

Rodney had new-found tolerance. "It could be a lie, Emma."

"It isn't though." Emma's face was still.

"How do you know?"

"Fred Darland stopped here the day he was killed. He wanted advice from me and Mother but she was visiting at the Starks' that day. Fred told me the whole story, how June had worried the life out of him since her mother died. It was June who made him move away from Buffalo Meadows. She said it was too lonely up there and she didn't like it.

"June is the one who offered to marry Max Roby if he would give her father land down here. Fred was too independent to take that kind of deal, even in a marriage arrangement, so he was going to prove up on the meadows and sign a relinquishment to Roby to pay him."

Rodney nodded. "That sounds like Fred Darland, all right."

"He didn't know about the will Roby had made—at least, he didn't mention it to me," Emma said. "When he stopped here, he had just quarreled bitterly with June because she'd told him she had no intentions of marrying Roby. Fred wanted to know how he could force her to go through with it, and I couldn't tell him. He was the most miserable man I've ever seen. I think he would have welcomed that shot on Squire's Hill if he had known it was coming."

Rodney shoved the coffee pot to the hot part of the stove. "Have you told anyone about this?"

"No, but I wish now I'd told your mother as soon as I knew."

"How'd the story get around?"

"Some people guessed at the truth, I suppose. Troy Clinton heard the quarrel June and her father had. Fred told me that. Maybe Clinton talked a little. Anyway, Roby died before he had a chance to know he had been tricked. The real reason he was at Old Agency was to get Shem Dudley to stand up for him. Shem was away and Roby waited for him to come back."

Emma's lack of emotion made the impact of her revelations all the heavier. Rodney had seen violence and dishonesty and he had been exposed to filth and deceit when he was growing up in boarding houses in New Orleans, in Natchez and in St. Louis, but the kind of rottenness June Darland had put on men's lives was beyond his understanding. It sickened him.

He said, "Do you suppose she lied again and sent Sq—those three men—after Roby because of the will?"

"I don't know."

165

"I think she did," Rodney said. "I've got to get Ma away from there."

"Your mother is a strong-willed woman. She admits her mistakes honestly, but she's at an age where it wouldn't be kindness to point them out to her. Don't worry, she'll see the truth in time, and that's when it will be all right for us to ask her to come home."

"What's the matter with a woman like June?" Rodney asked.

Emma shook her head.

Rodney thought of his mother, rough talking, rough acting, who was not afraid to walk before a crowd and embrace a madam she knew. Beside June Darland, Grandma Varnum was an innocent.

CHAPTER 17

On his way to break horses for Angus Copperwhaite, Ben Calistro stopped at the Y when Grandma Varnum, hanging washing on the line, hailed him and waved him in.

They exchanged greetings in Spanish. Grandma Varnum said, "Roped anybody lately, Bennie?"

Calistro raised his hands and eyes toward the sky. "I am a man of peace." They laughed together. "I go now to make gentle the horses for Señor Copperwhaite."

"He feeds good, but you won't get any pepper around his place. He's against spices and pepper."

"I will live." Calistro saw June come from the back door. She gave him a steady look and the hostility between them crackled across the space, but she was smiling when she walked over to talk to him. Calistro gave out his great politeness and withheld everything else.

"He's going over to bust horses for Angus," Grandma Varnum said.

"That's fine." June studied Calistro. "I have some horses here that should have been broken last year. I've always been afraid of riding, Mr. Calistro, but I think if I had a nice, gentle horse to start with, I might get over my fear. Would you be willing to break two or three horses for me, later?"

"I will be very busy," Calistro said.

"There's no hurry. Sometime when you don't have anything to do." June smiled. "*You* ask him, Grandma Varnum."

"Oh, he'll come down and do it some time," the old woman said. "I don't hold with women riding saddle horses, but if you want a couple of broomtails gentled, Bennie will do it when he has time. Won't you, Bennie?"

"There is no hurry," Calistro said. "Later, we will see."

He bowed and rode away, and he could remember every expression on the face of June Darland. She was a pale shadow on the desert when the sun was a torturing weight. She was like a cool, green thicket that promised much to a thirsty vaquero, but there would be no spring after he fought his way through the barbs and spines.

She was cruelty of spirit, and Calistro knew that quality well. She was kindness beckoning from a river in a peaceful valley, but when one went close, she receded into bleak, fanged mountains where Yaquis waited. She was a woman to hate, but since the woman of her left no stir in Ben Calistro, he could not have hated her enough to destroy her.

That task belonged to a lover, someone to put a gold cross between her breasts—and then to strangle her. But that was not the *gringo* way. Americans killed with fury, with much waste of strength, and with no appreciation whatever for their reasons.

Calistro spat the taste of June Darland from his mouth and went on to break his horses. Although horses were sometimes treacherous and often very stupid, there was much beauty in teaching them to do the task they were born to do.

Angus Copperwhaite would have questioned Calistro about his methods, about his experience; but Calistro answered not one question. He lifted his high shoulders in disdain and started to mount his broad-rumped pony.

"Wait a minute," Angus said.

"It is of no importance. If you have changed your mind about the horses—"

"I ain't changed my mind." Angus recognized the pride of a master workman. "Break the horses, Calistro, in your own way."

Angus went into the house to show that the matter was of no importance to him either. But he watched from the window when Calistro went to work. In a half hour he was satisfied that McQuiston was right: Calistro was a man for horses. And the price was a bargain.

The two men came to respect each other before the day was out. During the two weeks Calistro stayed at the ranch they became friends. Calistro soon understood that Angus was one who wanted something from other men, but it was all right, for Angus was willing, also, to give something in return. If he asked questions, he answered questions too.

One evening before supper when they were having their daily ritual of two drinks from the supply of whiskey in the big medicine chest Calistro confided the fact that he did not intend to stay in this north country beyond the next spring.

Angus was alarmed. "But McQuiston—"

"This is his land. He knows it now, and he will stay." It was a sadness, Calistro thought. Even though McQuiston was of his own village, born of a Creole mother whose family had been long in Mexico, the blood of his father was strong enough to send him north and to keep him away from the land of his birth.

To be a Mexican was a wonderful thing, and McQuiston had almost been one; but the only true way was to be born one.

"He's pretty strong on Miss Darland?" Angus asked. "What I mean is, how strong does he lean toward her?"

Calistro was far ahead. This was the business of a father looking toward his daughter's marriage. His respect for Angus increased. A father should always be watching carefully for the best match for his daughter. Girls were foolish. They talked of love, which was something hard to understand and of no great practical value.

"I do not speak of the Señorita Darland to McQuiston," Calistro said, "and when he speaks to me of her it is only to tell me that she is not as bad as I think."

Angus grunted. He knew he had an ally, but one who would not allow himself to be used.

They went to the house for supper. Watching Evaleth, Calistro gave the recent conversation with her father some thought, aware of the girl's interest whenever McQuiston's name was mentioned. Evaleth was indeed like an Aztec princess, but that meant nothing to one who could not see.

She was healthy. She obeyed her mother well. She understood many things about horses, which did not mean she would be a good wife, but Calistro liked her better because of the horses. If she loved McQuiston, that did no harm either. Her father had much land and was a shrewd man. He had asked many questions about McQuiston, even though it was clear that he had thought McQuiston a man from the very first.

It would be a good marriage.

But it was unlikely that it would occur. It was more likely that McQuiston would marry June Darland, if he could. Then when he knew what she was, because he was not a true Mexican, he would be unable to wipe out the disgrace.

He would be unable to kill her. He would only ride away and leave her. A *gringo* who did that was never the same afterward, seeing strange visions in the midst of friendly drinking, growing unreasonably angry with all women, never forgetting that he had been a fool.

If McQuiston were a Mexican, he could make his mistake and know what to do about it, and afterward be unhappy in the right way, without injuring the spirit. Calistro was sad, truly sad, about his great, good friend who was determined to bring unhappiness upon himself.

But there was nothing to be said about it, and nothing to be done. One did not tell his friend about a woman when the friend was unable to understand because he had a *gringo* head.

One afternoon Squanto came to the Copperwhaite place to tell Angus of some cattle that had strayed onto Squanto's range. The two men talked the matter over amiably, both watching Calistro as he worked with a savage blue roan that had been broken by quick, brutal methods a year before. The horse had injured two men who tried to ride him afterward, and then it had been turned loose.

Squanto knew the roan. He gave Angus a sharp look. Calistro put in a half hour with the animal and then he walked over to the rails. "That one is worth shooting," he told Angus.

"What's the matter with him?"

"He is worth a bullet only. I will go no farther with him." Calistro looked at Squanto. "He is like a woman who can never be changed. He is no good."

Squanto nudged Angus, grinning. "I said the same thing about that horse last year, remember?"

"I'll trade him off," Angus said.

Squanto laughed. "You'll have to take him clear out of the country to find a sucker." He turned to Calistro. "You want to come up to my place and bust some horses?"

After several moments of studying Squanto, Calistro

171

nodded. "But first there is something else to do, and so it will be next week before I come." This great man with the red hair had the face of honesty, and Calistro remembered that he had shot only into the high logs of the cabin at Buffalo Meadows. But of course there was no need to tell Squanto that the thing which must be done first was the taking of a horse from Van Buskirk.

On his way home Calistro stopped again at the Darland place. He was mildly surprised when he learned that Grandma Varnum was living there, not visiting. He was not surprised at all when he learned that McQuiston had been there several times to see June during the last two weeks.

Again June asked him to break some horses for her. Because Grandma Varnum repeated the request, Calistro gave his promise, but he left the time indefinite.

The cows were bunched at the upper end of the park when Calistro reached the basin. He went over to look at them. They were doing well and the pasture still retained its untouched appearance. It was beautiful but Calistro looked beyond it to another land where the heat and distance and the feel of life were more beautiful.

He was lonely. This was not coming home. He thought of winter as he rode to greet McQuiston.

They talked that night about Van Buskirk. McQuiston, not knowing, said things which told Calistro their paths were parting. "I talked to June about it, Ben. She finally admitted if we didn't do something, after sending word to Van Buskirk the way we did, we'd look foolish. I guess we'll have to get our horse."

At once Calistro thought less of the idea because June

172

Darland had approved it. A bitterness came to his face.

"You haven't changed your mind about it, have you?" McQuiston asked.

"No. We will do as we planned."

It took days of patient scouting, of waiting, but one morning they took their horses in a sliding descent down a narrow gulch and came out on the Tumbling road two hundred yards away from Billy Van Buskirk.

Van Buskirk reined in. He started to wheel his horse, but his pride was greater than his caution. Calistro and McQuiston waited. Van Buskirk came on up to meet them.

Billy Van Buskirk's worst mistake was allowing himself to be flanked. After that it was impossible to watch both McQuiston and Calistro. It occurred to him that he could drive straight between them and outrun them to Squanto's place, but his pride was too great for that.

McQuiston was pleasant. "You got our message?"

Van Buskirk stared at him and then shifted to watch Calistro.

"It's not too late to go back to your place and pick out a horse to replace the dun," McQuiston said.

"To hell with you!" Van Buskirk replied.

"That's what we thought." McQuiston smiled.

They were too easy, too sure, about the whole business. Van Buskirk had a moment of pure physical fear but there was nothing wrong with his courage. Calistro was not going to get a rope around his neck a second time. Van Buskirk stood up in the stirrups and started to draw his pistol.

Calistro had him covered in an instant. It was

173

McQuiston who threw the reata, up and over from where he held it ready against the skirt of his saddle. The loop drew tight around Van Buskirk's arms just above his elbows. With everything against him Van Buskirk still tried to get at his pistol. He nearly unseated himself in the struggle.

The pistol in Calistro's hand and the steady cruelness of Calistro's expression quieted Van Buskirk after a time.

McQuiston said, "There's still the chance for all of us to go to your place and pick out a horse."

"To hell with you!" Van Buskirk cried.

McQuiston jerked him from the steel-dust. They left him his rig. Calistro threw Van Buskirk's pistol into the willows by the creek. In a murderous rage Van Buskirk watched them put a hackamore on his horse.

"Any time you bring a packhorse up to the meadows, you can have the steel-dust back," McQuiston said. He and Calistro went down the road unhurriedly, towing Van Buskirk's favorite saddle horse.

Walking increased Van Buskirk's rage. By the time he reached home he had gone over a half dozen plans and none of them suited him. He saddled up another horse and went to see Avery Teague.

Teague listened to the story with the air of a magistrate whose mind is already made up. Even through the heat of his recital Van Buskirk saw a change in Teague, an air of moral decomposition, the pulsing of evil that had never been so apparent before. The man was as neat as ever, more composed than usual, but Van Buskirk sensed a seething behind the quietness.

"Why didn't you go see Squanto?" Teague asked.

"He's through with us. I know what he would have done. He would have laughed at me."

"He covers up a lot of things by laughing. They stole a horse. You can always go to the sheriff."

"What's the matter with you? You never talked like this before."

"No," Teague said. "But that was before Squanto pulled away from us, and before I got to thinking about him." His eyes held Van Buskirk in a narrow grip. "Squanto killed Fred Darland and Corbett. Now he's lost his guts for any kind of straight fighting."

"I don't believe that!"

Teague shrugged. "I'm sure of it. That's why I'm not going near the meadows. One day McQuiston will be knocked out of his saddle from the timber, or shot down some morning when he goes after a pail of water." Teague shook his head. "I don't want to be accused of it, and neither do you. The best thing you can do is take a packhorse up to those two and put yourself in the clear."

Van Buskirk was confused. The more he thought about Squanto, a man who was often strangely silent, a man who laughed sometimes when others saw no humor, the more he wondered if Teague was right. But there was the matter of the horse and Van Buskirk could not forget it.

"You're not going to help me then, Teague?"

Teague shook his head. "Not by going straight to the meadows and winding up being accused of another murder."

"Who accused you of any?"

"Charlie Nye—practically."

"Oh hell! He talked to me too about Corbett. He didn't say that."

"He hasn't forgotten Roby, either," Teague said.

Remembrance of Los Pinos clawed at Van Buskirk but he stuck to the subject of the horse.

"They took it for bait," Teague said. "Don't fall for their trap. Buffalo Meadows can wait."

"Are you going to help me or not?"

Teague shook his head. "I've got my own worries. What makes Squanto so sure he's going to marry June? I tell you he's got a bucketful of tricks that—"

"I came here to talk about my horse!"

"Sorry, Billy." Teague shook his head.

A bleakness settled in Van Buskirk as he rode away. He was done with Teague and done with Squanto. He wished fervently that the three of them had never got together that day on Los Pinos.

Teague called that evening on June Darland. He had to wait until three miners who had stopped to eat and stay overnight at the Y finished their meal and went to the bunkhouse with Clinton.

Grandma Varnum sensed the coming showdown. She said, "I'll do the dishes and clean up, June."

Teague closed the door behind her when she went into the kitchen. He turned on June. "When are we going to get married? If not, I want to know that too. Now."

June seemed surprised. "I don't remember ever saying I'd marry you."

"Don't play with me about it! You've kept me coming here a long time. Now I'm due to be answered one way or another. I won't wait any longer."

Teague's intensity warned the woman. He was dangerous. She had always been able to stall him off before, but tonight would not be so easy. She knew how wise she had been in never offering this man the chance she had offered McQuiston after the dance at the schoolhouse.

She said, "You're rushing things, Avery."

"It's time I did. Squanto has something up his sleeve, and you're seeing too much of McQuiston. When are—"

"McQuiston has done something no one else ever did. He's holding Buffalo Meadows." June watched Teague's sharp reaction and knew how to proceed.

"He'll lose the park."

"Like Corbett, Avery?"

Teague's face turned white.

June spoke slowly. "You scared me the night you jumped on McQuiston after he'd licked Squanto. It wasn't fair, Avery. So now I'm mixed up. I don't know just what to think about you. I've always liked you a lot, maybe even more than a lot, but after that night—"

"I lost my temper, that was all. I never was afraid of McQuiston. Maybe I couldn't beat him in a fist fight but that's a stupid way of fighting. I wouldn't have got into it if I hadn't lost my temper. You saw what happened the first day he came. He backed away from me."

"I saw it, but I'm not sure he backed away."

"He wouldn't fight!"

"Are you sure, Avery?" June's voice was low.

They kept looking at each other. Teague said, "You

mean I'm afraid of him?"

"I don't know. And not necessarily him—I don't mean that. After the night you jumped on him when he was already finished, I've never been sure about you. Before that—well, I always thought you weren't afraid of anyone."

"I'm not and you know it!"

"I don't mean McQuiston," June said. "I mean anyone. I'm not sure, and I won't marry a man unless I am sure he has courage." She watched Teague steadily. "That's all the answer I can give you right now, Avery."

"What do you expect me to do?"

"Nothing! Did I say you should do anything? All I said was that I'm not sure about you." June turned away. She smiled as she went toward the kitchen to help Grandma Varnum. Before she opened the door her expression had changed to one of quiet sadness.

Teague went out without saying good-night. He remembered the day of Fred Darland's death, when he had stopped here. June had been a different woman then, not so sure of herself, not so skilled at digging straight to where it hurt inside a man.

She had been almost hysterical as she told him how her father had beaten her after she refused to marry Roby. She had been an injured child then, crying out her wrongs, raging wildly against her father's cruelty and deceit.

Teague remembered the day very well.

Now he went up the road with doubts of himself festering in his mind all the worse because June knew them too. Yes, it had been a mistake to finish McQuiston that night. By doing so he had made himself less than a man in June's eyes.

With uncanny insight she had gone back to the source, the day Teague had tried to make a pistol fight with McQuiston. Tonight she had thrown the failure of that, too, in Teague's face, at the same time holding out a promise.

He was being used. Teague knew it. But he was being used along lines that were already in his mind. He wanted June too much to care. He had done something which appeared cowardly to her; now she had given him the chance to redeem himself.

It was simple. He would finish what he had started the first day he saw McQuiston, and it would be proof to June. In a fair fight he would kill McQuiston. The simplicity of the idea grew more attractive. One stroke would remove McQuiston and set Teague far above his other two rivals in June's estimation; and it would reopen the way to Buffalo Meadows.

The sound of a horse up the road sent Teague off to the side. He drew his pistol and waited in the darkness under cottonwoods. But the other rider was not deaf. He sent a careless, booming hail down the road.

It was Squanto. Teague answered and went back to the road to wait. Peering hard through the starlight, he saw no glint of a pistol belt buckle on Squanto's middle. The fool went unarmed through the dark as if he owned the country. Carelessness? No. Part of some clever design.

"Are you holding it against me for what I did on the day of the drive?" Squanto asked.

During a sober moment, when the heat was out of

him, Teague had admitted to himself the fact that Squanto had been right, but he was never going to tell Squanto that. "I haven't exactly forgotten what you did."

"Suit yourself." Squanto paused. "You must have left the Y early."

"I wasn't run off, if that's what you mean."

"Your temper is going to bite you someday," Squanto said cheerfully. "Was McQuiston there?"

"You mean I left because of McQuiston. God—"

"Hold it, hold it. I wanted to ask him when his partner is coming down to break some horses for me. The idiot who tried the last time—"

"You're pretty friendly with those two, ain't you?"

"No," Squanto said. "I'm just reasonable." He started to ride on.

"Wait a minute. I got a question or two."

Squanto waited.

"Have you asked June to marry you?"

"That's nice and personal," Squanto said, "but since I ain't never asked her, I'll tell you."

"Yeah. I imagine you've never asked her."

"None at all. When I do, I figure to make it stick." Squanto laughed and rode away.

Teague sat unmoving for a time, distrusting the laughter, distrusting the night.

He did not sleep well when he went home. It was like other times when the darkness of his mind unloosed specters, like the week following Los Pinos. He remembered June's hysterical weeping the day her father was killed. The house creaked and he sat up in bed, straining to see danger creeping in on him. Once he thought he

180

heard out in the road horses of men coming after him.

Grandma Varnum looked hard at June when Teague left without saying good-night. "What'd you do to him?"

"I told him he was a coward."

"Do you mean you worked on him to make trouble?"

"No! I wouldn't do that again."

"I'm not so sure you realize what goes on in a man's mind, let alone your own."

"Do *you*?" June asked.

"I've had some practice with men."

"Oh?" June was smiling, but there lay behind her expression an intelligent, searching curiosity that made Grandma Varnum wish she had kept still. "What kind of—"

"Never mind," the old woman said. For all of June's living back here in the hills, she was sharper than she ought to be.

Later, in the living room, the old woman said, "June, you've got to settle things among those three, or tell them all not to come here. You've—"

"Three? Don't you include Dallas McQuiston?"

"Him too." Grandma Varnum studied June's satisfied expression. "Has he asked you to marry him?"

"Not yet."

June's smugness was wearing on Grandma Varnum. "But you're sure he will?"

"Yes." June nodded.

"Will you want him if he does ask?"

"I'll wait and see." June laughed.

"You and me had better have a little showdown about some things, June. In the first place—"

Squanto's arrival interrupted Grandma Varnum's lecture. He settled into a chair and had little to say, except to give slow answers to questions, or to rumble with heavy humor when June tried to tease him. He stayed less than an hour and when he was gone, there seemed to have been no reason for his visit.

"I like him better than Teague, I think," June said. "You know something—I'm a little afraid of Avery at times."

"If you ask me, which you don't seem to want to, I'd say Squanto is the one you'd better be afraid of. He's not going to stand for any shenanigans, and he's never going to take no for an answer."

"You seem to know a lot about men. Just how did you learn so much, Grandma Varnum?"

"Never you mind, June. Just pay some attention to what I say." Grandma Varnum went to bed. It surprised her to realize she was beginning to long for her son's home. It was noisy there, what with the girls always going a mile a minute, and sometimes there were sharp little disagreements over methods of raising children; but Grandma Varnum had never felt so tuckered out at the end of each day, or so vague and worried about the next day.

There was tension at the Y all the time, even when June and Grandma Varnum were the only ones there.

Ready for bed, June stopped in the doorway of the old woman's room. "Do you think that's right about Squanto—he won't take no for an answer?"

"I know it is." Maybe it was not quite so. Squanto had tremendous stubbornness, but there was also tremendous reason in him. Still, it wouldn't hurt June a bit to begin understanding that all men were not easily handled.

"But what if I decided to marry someone else?"

"There might be a shooting, if you didn't handle things right."

"Why, that would be terrible!"

"Yeah," Grandma Varnum said. Maybe June was learning something after all. "Now go away and let me sleep."

"You always liked Billy Van Buskirk better than any of the others, didn't you, Grandma?"

"I still do, but I ain't arranging marriages. Now go away and let me get some rest."

CHAPTER 18

Van Buskirk heard that Calistro was breaking horses at the Bissell place, and so Van Buskirk went there on the run to settle a score. "I considered him," Homer Bissell said, "after what Angus Copperwhaite told me, but he won't be here until after he does some work for Squanto. He ought to be up there now."

In view of Squanto's recent behavior, Van Buskirk was not sure of how Squanto would receive him and his mission. But that was something to be handled when it came. The memory of Calistro's deftness with a pistol was another troubling thought, even to a reckless man. But there was the matter of the horse and no honorable way to end the matter, except by force.

Van Buskirk went back up the road to find Calistro. He did not intend to stop at the Y. June was working in her garden near the spring behind the bunkhouse. She waved him in. Van Buskirk had his mind on killing a man; it was some time before the drift of the conversation took full effect on him.

"You've asked me a dozen times to marry you, Billy."

"I guess that's so."

They were sitting on a bench beside the spring. June was quiet, her hands in her lap. She gave Van Buskirk a full stare and then she lowered her eyes. "Have you given up trying, Billy?"

"Why, no—I—" It was several moments before Van Buskirk could believe the truth. "Will you marry me?"

The woman nodded.

Van Buskirk was beside himself with joy. He leaped up and pulled June to her feet. Long afterward he was puzzled by the fierce hunger of the woman's kiss, but at the moment he read no more than his own excitement into it.

"There's one thing I want you to do, Billy."

"Name it!"

"Settle your trouble with Calistro and McQuiston. We wouldn't want to start out with that hanging over our heads. I'd be worried all the time."

It was so simple Van Buskirk wondered why he had not considered it before: All he had to do was replace the dun. It was his fault that it was dead. But there was still a problem.

"What about the meadows? You've told me how

you've always wanted—"

"No. Forget the meadows too. There's been too much trouble over them. We'll start brand-new, Billy."

They talked it over, Van Buskirk hardly knowing what he said. June made him agree to keep the secret until she had a chance to tell Squanto and Teague as gently as she could; and then they would have a celebration to announce the wedding date.

They went to tell Grandma Varnum. The old woman was so happy she almost cried, but she concealed her feelings with a bluster of roughness. When she heard that June had made Van Buskirk promise to settle his trouble with McQuiston and Calistro, she decided it had been worth coming to the Y.

Van Buskirk left at a gallop. June waved at him, smiling. Turning away, Grandma Varnum missed the edge of something bright and cruel.

In the shade of trees at the end of the bunkhouse Troy Clinton sat at a weathered plank table and stared at a saddle he had been repairing. Years of knowing too much weighed heavily on him. He was a man of bitter memories, tightly held. For a long time he had loved June like a daughter, amazed, sometimes tickled to his very depths, by the things she did.

He was a survivor of seven years of trail drives up from Texas and he had been through other brutal mills, so that now there was little left in him to make for condemnation of anyone's actions. He had seen June stack the deck and make complete fools of men and he had watched with sardonic interest; but this last act of hers was running something in him too thin to hold out much longer. There was nothing he cared to do about it for others. All he could do for himself was to saddle up and drift away.

Maybe he would tell Squanto, the only man he had ever talked to fully about other matters on the Tumbling. And maybe he would not.

His decision to leave was about half made when June gave him orders to carry the news of the celebration around the Tumbling country. She talked to him like he was an unpaid servant, but he was used to that. Habit was strong. He went to carry out her orders.

He derived a mordant sort of humor from the reactions of people as he rode around the country. He knew that a great many of those who told him they would be unable to attend the festivities would be there if for no other reason than curiosity. A blowout at the Y, with invitations to everyone, could mean just one thing: June was going to get married at last.

Clinton extended nothing but the invitation, silently admiring June's keenness. She knew the power of curiosity, and she knew that marriage, no matter who were the principals, was something that women must defend with approval. When he returned to the Y after a two-day trip he delivered the information to June that her celebration would not suffer from lack of attendance.

"You told McQuiston?"

Clinton nodded.

"How did he take it?"

"He said thanks."

"I mean is he coming?"

"I reckon," Clinton said.

"What about Avery Teague?"

"He'll be here."

On the evening of the day Squanto received news of the coming celebration he went to the Y faster than he usually traveled. There was haste in his manner after he arrived and a tenseness that disturbed Grandma Varnum. She wondered if, after all, she was right about a powerful determination in Squanto that would not allow him to lose June.

Grandma Varnum had no chance to hear what went on, for Squanto said, "Let's walk around outside, June."

June put a shawl around her shoulders and went outside with Squanto. Cold starlight gave his face a brutal look. He was not Teague, whose temper could be used against him, or Van Buskirk, who was a simpleton. June was all at once completely frightened.

Squanto said, "Why'd you tell Van Buskirk you'd marry him?"

June took in a sharp breath. Her defenses began to work. "Did Billy tell you?"

Clinton had told but that was of no importance. "Who do you think you're taking in by having Billy make peace with McQuiston?" Squanto said. "It ain't going to be enough to hide behind."

"I'm going back inside."

"Shut up and listen. You told Van Buskirk you'd marry him. Now you expect me to kill him or Teague to kill him. It's a filthy trick, June—another Roby trick—but it won't work."

"Is marrying him a filthy trick, Uncle Squanto?"

"I know you, June. By now you ought to realize that, so let's not waste time with lies."

"I'm not lying. At the barbecue we'll announce—"

"You can do better than that," Squanto said.

"What do you mean?"

"You can marry him at the celebration. I'm going to bring a preacher. I'll have men covering Teague and McQuiston so they can't even look cross-eyed at Billy. Folks will be clamoring for the minister to perform a ceremony after I work on them a little. Billy will be all for it too. You know Billy, he don't like to wait for anything.

"Instead of the fight you're trying to rig up, you'll have a marriage on your hands. People will be remembering about Roby. It won't be easy to back out."

"I'll have Billy shoot you!"

Squanto sighed. "How can he be mad, with me bringing the preacher and yelling for the two of you to get married?"

June cursed Squanto with words he had never heard her use. He reached out at last and slapped her, trying to do it lightly. The blow rocked her sidewise. "No wife of mine is going to use language like that."

"Wife! Your wife!" June tried scorn then and it broke on Squanto like smoke against a rock.

She recognized the fact and changed pace again. "But you've never asked me to marry you, Squanto."

"I will, after you've got a few things straightened out. I know what you are and I'm the only man who'll ever be able to stomach you, because I love you in spite of knowing what you are." For a second time Squanto showed a trace of humility, the quality in a man that was despicable to June Darland.

But the truth made her afraid of him, and the fact that he could love her, guessing as much about her as he had, aroused her hatred. "Bring your minister," she said, "and see whether I back out or not."

"All right."

June played her bluff out in a long stare. In the pale starlight she saw the grin on Squanto's face. "You would bring him, wouldn't you! Damn you!"

"I'm going to." Squanto turned to go toward his horse.

"Wait!" June ran to him. "What am I going to do?"

"Tell Billy the truth."

"I can't!" It was a wail. "I did lie, Squanto, but what am I going to do now?"

"I'll tell you one thing you're *not* going to do, June. Billy is up in the hills and he won't be back until the day of the barbecue. There'll be no use to send Clinton after him, because I'll stop him. You're not going to rig a fight between Billy and me by telling more lies."

"Don't bring a minister. I'll find some way of telling Billy as soon as he shows up here."

"I'll be watching that." Squanto strode off and mounted his horse. He rode away, trembling and sweating in the cold night. Twice now he had staked everything on a bluff. He had a bad moment of wondering if he would have to live his whole life that way after he and June were married.

But no, once they were married, she would settle down. She would have to. The memory of slapping her scared him, for he had never struck a woman in his life.

CHAPTER 19

Dressed in their Sunday best, McQuiston and Calistro came down from Buffalo Meadows in the middle of the afternoon on the day of the barbecue. McQuiston was silent, looking now and then to find some slanting mockery on Calistro's face; but the Mexican was carrying his private thoughts with dignity.

She must have decided on a man; it was the only construction McQuiston could put on the event at the Y.

And now that it was so, he wanted her badly, for losing her made her twice as desirable. He had been too slow and cautious, too afraid of himself in a matter he had never approached before. He should have gone to her as soon as he got the news, but his pride had been offended and he had not acted. Now it was too late.

Yet he would not admit that it was too late.

He was in a dark mood when he and Calistro reached the Y. He wanted to see June at once, but a glance at the house told him not to rush. The porch was crowded with women. Others, just arriving, were going toward it, bearing food and advice and a sharp curiosity.

Children were storming around the out-buildings, shouting as they dashed across the yard. Men were scattered everywhere in small groups, talking loudly, laughing. Some of them, McQuiston thought sourly, were no doubt making bets. A poker game was going on in the bunkhouse. On the hill below the spring Dan and Mark Copperwhaite were tending the dripping carcass of a steer over a pit of coals. Homer Bissell was supervising.

McQuiston walked past washtubs of coffee brewing over open fires beside plank tables in the yard. He went to the barbecue pit and said to Bissell, "I made a mistake at the schoolhouse, Bissell."

Bissell smeared his hands across his apron. He reached out with a powerful grip. "I've slapped that kid a few times myself for shooting off his trap." He grinned. "How do you like the smell of that beef?"

"Great. Save me a hind quarter." McQuiston glanced toward the house. "Who's the lucky man?"

Bissell stared. "It ain't you then? By God, I guess it ain't, from the look of your face." He shook his head. "Squanto denies it. Van Buskirk says it ain't him. That leaves Teague, and he ain't here yet."

McQuiston discovered how hard it was to smile, but he managed it. He put his hand on Mark's shoulder and said, "I guess the two of us aren't much good, are we?"

The implication that he had been a serious contender startled the youth. It raised his standing, made him feel that he and McQuiston were sharing a common loss. Mark Copperwhaite's dislike of McQuiston died on the spot.

"Did your folks come over, Mark?" McQuiston asked.

"Ev and Ma. Pa had business on the range and couldn't get back in time."

"Angus sent this here beef though," Bissell said. He grinned to himself and his thought was evident: Angus had a marriageable daughter and was happy to contribute to an event that would put a few young men back in circulation.

On his way across the yard McQuiston met Billy Van Buskirk, excited, hurrying. They nodded and let it stand at that. Although the affair of the dun was settled now, cordial relations would be long in coming, if ever.

A buggy pulled into the yard and a man helped his wife down. She looked around sharply. "Well, I must say she hasn't got whiskey barrels set up all over the place. That's a little something in her favor, I suppose."

"She won't have it around," the man said. He winked at McQuiston. "But if you're dead set on having a drink, Ma, I'll rustle up Tom Hosmer. Never knew him to go on a blowout without a jug or two."

"Bring them pies and don't be so smart!"

Squanto was moving slowly from one group of men to another. He stopped in front of McQuiston. "Have any trouble in your system?"

"Make it plain, Squanto."

"It's a barbecue, not a fighting bee."

"Who started the last fight here?"

"Sort of edgy, huh, McQuiston? Suit yourself, but today nobody's going to make a fight, not you or anyone else."

"Who's she marrying?" McQuiston asked.

"I didn't know she was figuring to marry anyone," Squanto said, and went toward the house.

McQuiston saw him stop to speak to Evaleth on the porch. She said something with a smile and Squanto shook his head, grinning. Squanto tried to go inside and a flurry of women turned him back. He went, instead, to the other end of the porch and looked up the road.

Much was being forgiven here today, or at least over-looked, but it would not take much to upset things. McQuiston knew that he himself was carrying trouble, but he tried to set himself against it. He wanted to see June; he wanted the truth.

He kept watching Squanto. If Squanto had set himself up as the peace-keeper, he was making no mistake by watching the road for Teague.

"Does it hurt?" Evaleth was beside McQuiston, speaking before he knew she was there.

McQuiston studied her a moment. She seemed angry about something. He said, "I suppose it does."

"You know very well it does."

"All right, have it that way. Does it make you happy, Evaleth?"

"No. And not sorry for you either. You have a high opinion of yourself, Dallas McQuiston, but you're just as stupid as any other man I know." Evaleth watched his face with a frankness that was irritating.

McQuiston shook his head. This girl had something on her mind but she was going at it vaguely. He saw mixed anger and appeal and it lifted her from being pretty to being beautiful. He glanced at the house. If June did not come outside soon, he would go in to find her.

"Are you interested in who June's going to marry?" Evaleth asked.

"Do you know?"

"I know what she told me to tell you," Evaleth said.

"It's second-hand information, of course, and by the time you get to see her, she may have changed her mind."

"You're not being very kind, or even polite."

"I don't intend to be."

"Who is the man?" McQuiston asked.

Evaleth's mimicry was biting. " 'Please, dear Evaleth, will you tell Mr. McQuiston for me? I just can't bring myself to face him today. Will you tell him as gently as you can that I've decided to marry Mr. Teague?' "

"Teague!" McQuiston stared angrily at the house.

"That's what she said."

It must be so. There was Squanto watching the road, with his mind set on forestalling trouble.

"Have you seen Van Buskirk?" Evaleth asked.

The question came through slowly to McQuiston. "Van Buskirk and I don't have any quarrel."

"I didn't mean that. Have you seen him?"

"I saw him, yes!"

"Didn't he look unusually happy?"

"I didn't notice."

Evaleth's eyes narrowed. "I don't know where men keep their brains." She walked away.

A few moments later McQuiston saw June come outside. He strode toward her, oblivious of the crowd and noise. A boy looking back over his shoulder as he ran crashed head-on against McQuiston's stomach and started to fall. Without looking at him, McQuiston reached down to steady him, and then he went on toward the porch.

"June!" McQuiston stopped on the ground at the end

of the porch away from Squanto. "June, can I see you?"

Squanto heard the call and turned. The women on the porch heard. A silence came upon them. But it seemed that June had not heard. Then one of the women touched June's shoulder and spoke to her and nodded toward McQuiston.

Slowly June walked along the porch until she stood at the end, looking down at McQuiston. She had never appeared so desirable to him as she was at the moment.

"Didn't Evaleth tell you, Dallas?"

"I'll hear it from you."

June's face was pale. The orange-brown eyes were steady.

"Yes, it's Teague."

They were watching and listening hard on the porch. McQuiston kept his voice low, cursing the fact that there were spectators. "But him, June! My God—"

"You never gave me any indication of your intentions, Dallas. It could have been different if . . ." June shook her head, smiling wistfully. "Sometimes decisions are more or less forced on a person." There was a pathetic sadness in her expression.

"Who forced anything on you?"

June raised her voice. "Nobody, Dallas. I didn't say that. Now please don't cause him any trouble. Have a good time here today but don't make any trouble."

The woman walked back along the porch. McQuiston was a disappointed suitor and she had pleaded with him to behave himself. The women approved. They gave McQuiston sharp looks and one of them put her arm around June and said, "There, there, dear, you did the right thing."

Squanto came around the back corner of the house. He spoke faster than usual and his manner showed unaccustomed strain. "What did she tell you, McQuiston?"

"What business is it of yours?"

Squanto grabbed McQuiston's arm and hauled him away from the end of the porch, over against the house where they could not be overheard. McQuiston had no chance to struggle before Squanto let go and said, "I've got to know what she told you!"

Tom Hosmer was carrying a jug into the bunkhouse. A group of men trailing with him were talking loudly. Out of their overall noise came Van Buskirk's clear laughter.

"I want to know what she told you!" Squanto said, and McQuiston knew the man's patience was breaking.

"She told me not to start any trouble." McQuiston watched Van Buskirk go into the bunkhouse. Considering he was another rejected suitor, Van Buskirk was in high good spirits. What had Evaleth been trying to get at?

"That's good advice, coming from her," Squanto said. "Who'd she say she was going to marry?"

"I didn't know she was going to marry anyone. Isn't that what you told me a while ago?" McQuiston walked away. He almost bumped into Calistro. "Never mind, Ben, I don't need any help."

Calistro shrugged. He looked at Squanto and fell in beside McQuiston.

June is right. I had no claim on her and I shied away

196

when I could have spoken up. The memory of June's sad look when she said things could have been different twisted pain in McQuiston.

"She's marrying Teague, Ben. Like a damned fool I stalled around too long."

"Shall we go home?"

McQuiston shook his head. He might even yet get another chance to talk alone to June, to get her to change her mind. There would be hell to pay then, but his recklessness was ready for it and he had already a debt to collect from Avery Teague.

"There was once when you did not wish to shoot a man here to keep this woman from having disgrace in her yard," Calistro said.

"I'll make no trouble if I can avoid it."

"That will not be simple," Calistro said. "Teague is coming now."

Teague dismounted just inside the gate. He led his horse from there, working his way slowly through the crowd, a slender, neatly dressed man who paused often to smile and exchange a few words with his neighbors of the Tumbling country.

And all the while his eyes were searching, looking beyond the people he talked to. He saw McQuiston and this time passed him over casually. There was not even a broken instant of fixed stare, but Calistro murmured, "You will not avoid trouble. From the first day we came to this place—"

But McQuiston had turned away, going toward the back door of the house to find June.

He got as far as the kitchen, and there women as determined as he turned him back. "She's resting in her room," one of them said. "You'll not disturb her."

"I've got to see her."

They had heard what June had told him on the porch. They were formidable and McQuiston could not pass unless he used force. "Tell her I want to talk to her before she announces anything."

"We'll do that," one of the women said, and McQuiston knew that it would not be done. He went outside.

Squanto was waiting for him. "Don't even think about making a pass at Van Buskirk, McQuiston."

"Van Buskirk? Mind your own business."

"I am," Squanto said. He watched McQuiston walk away. Things were going wrong and Squanto was not sure of what to do. June was outwitting him. She hadn't told the truth to Van Buskirk, he was sure; and he didn't know what she had told McQuiston.

He wished now that he had brought the minister; but he had been afraid to carry the bluff that far.

It started and ended where a group was watching Tom Hosmer and Jerry Stark pitching horseshoes for a dollar a game behind the bunkhouse. "I can beat any man that throws for close!" Hosmer said, and made his second pitch. The shoe clanged around the pin and fell off on top of one of Stark's. There was an argument. Dan Copperwhaite, measuring with a stick, said, "I give the point to Tom."

"I got him by a quarter of an inch!" Stark protested. "Measure that again."

McQuiston was watching without interest. Dan measured. He looked up at McQuiston. "How about it? Right there where my thumb is—"

"Don't ask him, Copperwhaite. He'd cheat both of them." Avery Teague was standing near the other pin. He had taken off his black coat. "McQuiston would steal his grandmother's last pipeful of tobacco."

The tone of Teague's words, the way he stood with the wildness flickering behind his eyes, told everyone all that was necessary. The men close to McQuiston moved aside quickly.

McQuiston and Teague faced each other across the distance between the two pins, roughly forty feet. Suddenly McQuiston's anger was gone and he wished that the affair had not come to a head here at the Y. Teague was the man June had picked to marry. No matter what happened now, she would be injured.

To the last moment McQuiston tried to protect June Darland. He said, "Still sore about Buffalo Meadows, I see." After that there was no use to say more, no time to think of anyone but himself. A man stood ready to kill him, no longer Avery Teague, no longer any man, but a deadliness that would move quickly, a threat as fundamental as a charging animal or a coiled, venomous serpent.

McQuiston lived one long, cool instant after he sensed the sharp movement of the threat.

He was drawing his pistol and aiming it as he would have pointed his finger and firing without any sense of haste. Time was nothing. Each action lay distinctly separate in his mind, but only for the instant, and then they blended and were lost and afterward there would be no memory except result.

Nothing was sure until McQuiston saw Teague's reaction from the terrible blow. The man hunched his shoulders and lowered his head. Both arms came down and Teague fell beside the iron pin.

McQuiston stood with the bitter odor of the cartridge in his nose, with the muzzle of his pistol dipping to cover the figure on the ground. Squanto came into view, obscuring the picture as he reached down to Teague. Then others ran to crowd in beside Squanto.

Calistro was beside McQuiston, his liquid eyes on the men around Teague, his gaze shifting to watch the faces of the men running toward the scene. "Now is the time to go home?"

"I want to talk to June, Ben. I want to tell her . . ." What was it he could say? *I've killed the man you were going to marry, but it wasn't my fault.*

McQuiston and Calistro moved against the traffic of people running from all parts of the yard. June was on the porch with a group of women. McQuiston heard her say, "Avery? Oh, no!" and it was a cry of anguish that lanced into him.

He changed direction and went toward the corrals.

He was leading his horse from the corral and a crowd of excited boys were gaping at him when Evaleth came to him and said, "I'm sorry."

She was not angry then. She looked at McQuiston quietly, with her sympathy a strong, honest quality. McQuiston was puzzled. "Is he dead?"

"No, but they say he won't live."

"Why be sorry for me then?"

"I am," Evaleth said. "For you and Van Buskirk. Squanto is different. He knows."

"Knows what?"

Evaleth glanced at Calistro. His face was impassive. He gave her a tiny headshake and she walked away without another look at McQuiston.

Going across the yard, McQuiston heard a woman say, "I knew it, I knew it! This place is a curse." She turned to a girl at her side. "Go find your father, Mary. We're going home."

On the way to Buffalo Meadows, Calistro said, "On the day we saw him the first time, we knew you would have to kill him. It was his fault he is dying."

"But I hurt her by doing it. Why did she have to pick Teague?"

"Would it have been easier to kill Squanto or Van Buskirk? Squanto is a man of great courage, one I like. Van Buskirk is a foolish boy, but he is learning. I, myself, would not find it pleasant to kill either of them, but Teague . . ." Calistro shrugged.

"Why did she pick the one man that I was bound to have trouble with?"

McQuiston had answered the question even as he spoke it, but Calistro saw that his friend did not know the fact. If a man like Squanto, who was very slow and very shrewd, did not understand the truth about the woman, then how could the truth be forced on McQuiston?

Perhaps Squanto did know about the woman and did not care. It would be very strange if a *gringo* could be like that but maybe it was possible.

Like the green valley of the cool water was this woman, waving to those dying of the thirst; but when they came close she was gone into the bleak, fanged mountains and even then there were those, like Teague, who would follow her to their deaths. Those who learned to turn back by their own effort could defeat the madness, but if they were restrained by others, the dream of beauty that did not exist would always lie in their minds like a mirage.

Benevides Calistro held his silence.

CHAPTER 20

The last words McQuiston had spoken to Teague, the effort to base their quarrel on Buffalo Meadows, held back only for a time the weight of censure that fell on June Darland. Too many people remembered that this was the second time a man who was to marry her had met violence at the hands of her other suitors.

From June herself there came no direct statement that Teague was the man she had planned to marry, but after he was carried into the house, she wept over him so bitterly and then went into a state of shock, that it became quite clear he was her choice.

Grandma Varnum and a few other women who had worked before against the end result of pistol fights were doing all they could for Teague, and a few others who had not yet caught the full impact of unease the affair had caused were trying to comfort June. Van Buskirk and Squanto had herded all curious men out of the house.

Grandma Varnum was suspicioning things that had risen in her mind before. June's state of shock came under her hard scrutiny, following as it had a long outburst of crying; that was not quite the natural sequence in Grandma Varnum's experience.

Mark and Dan Copperwhaite had gone for a doctor. It was a gesture that must be made, but Grandma Varnum was sure that Teague would last only a few hours. The celebration, of course, was ruined. Homer Bissell looked sourly at the beef, which still needed two hours more to be right. His wife came over and told him it was time to go home.

"It was your idea to come," Bissell said.

"Maybe it was, but there's been no change at this place. Everything that woman does causes murder. Round up the kids and let's get out of here. After what happened at the schoolhouse that night, I'm surprised that I ever was silly enough to come here today."

The more outraged visitors left early. Others stayed on longer to receive the news of Teague's death. Squanto and Van Buskirk sat on the porch, Van Buskirk staring glumly at his boots. He thought that June should have made some forthright statement to counteract the talk he'd overheard about Teague being the man she was supposed to marry. Of course she had been upset, hardly hearing anything Van Buskirk said when he tried to talk to her.

He saw Squanto watching him with an odd expression. It was like the day on the hill when their plan to scatter McQuiston's herd had fizzled out. "What's the matter with you?" Van Buskirk asked irritably.

203

"Nothing, Billy. It's just that I got fooled. I sort of expected the trouble to be around you."

"Yeah, I suppose." Van Buskirk shook his head. "That damned McQuiston . . ."

"Avery was bought and paid for, Billy, as far as McQuiston was concerned. Avery asked for it the first time we ever saw McQuiston, and he cinched it when he used his boots on McQuiston. But I should have guessed—"

Squanto did not finish his thought. "Guessed what?" Van Buskirk asked.

Squanto looked at the men still waiting. He rose and went into the yard. "You may as well all go home, boys. There's nothing you can do here. Teague will be gone in an hour or so."

It was almost sunset when June came outside. She looked at the deserted yard, the tables set up for a feast that had never been. The beef was still hanging over the pit. Clinton came out of the bunkhouse and trudged over to the pit. He tipped his shoulders sidewise as he dug into his pocket for a heavy claspknife.

He cut a piece of meat from a hind quarter and carried it back into the bunkhouse.

"They're all gone? Everybody is gone?" June asked in a wondering tone.

Squanto watched her coolly. Van Buskirk leaped up. "June, I want to—"

She waved him away with a tragic gesture. "I can't talk to you now, Billy, not about anything between us. Everything is changed now. I feel as terrible as I did when poor Max—" She put her face into her hands and began to cry.

Van Buskirk rushed to console her. Squanto stared off into the distance.

"It'll be all right, June," Van Buskirk said. "We'll get married and go away from here. We'll forget all about—"

"No, no!" June said. "I can't ask you to do that. I can't ask you to share the misery I've caused."

Squanto turned to look at June in cold admiration. It might even be that she was sincere, but he saw her eyes when she looked over Van Buskirk's shoulder. Behind her show of misery was a calculating expression.

Grandma Varnum came out. She watched June for a few moments. "He's asking for you, June."

"I can't see him! I couldn't stand it."

"Maybe he wants to make a will." Squanto was half musing and his tone carried great weariness.

Van Buskirk turned on him savagely. "What kind of talk is that?"

Squanto ignored him. "We'd all better go in. We were his friends once."

Teague was dying hard. "You damned vultures," he whispered, looking at Squanto and Van Buskirk. "You're happy now, ain't you?"

"No, Avery." A distant bleakness marked Squanto's manner. "I can't say that we're happy."

"Get out," Teague said. "I want to talk to June."

Van Buskirk started to turn away, but Squanto put out his arm and stopped him. "There's nothing you can tell her that we don't know already, Avery."

June tried to shove Squanto toward the door. "He

wants to talk to me." Squanto pushed her hands aside without looking at her. She appealed to Grandma Varnum. "Make them leave!"

Grandma Varnum stared at June with harsh old eyes and made no move.

"He wants to tell us he killed Corbett," Squanto said, "but we knew that."

"You guessed it," Teague said. "You couldn't have known it."

"Get out!" June cried. "Leave him alone."

"He wants to tell us that he shot your father," Squanto said, "but we knew that too."

Van Buskirk was pale and sick looking.

"He did no such thing!" June said. "You didn't, did you, Avery?"

Teague's face was gray and thin and sharp. His eyes moved slowly and fixed on June and the accusation in them was like a scream, but he did not speak again. He held his secretive spirit to the last, his fading gaze set in terrible bitterness on the woman's face.

Afterward, Grandma Varnum sat down in the living room. All her age was in her face. Squanto and Van Buskirk were out on the porch. She heard their voices but what they said no longer interested her.

"You were another Roby," Squanto was saying. "She wasn't going to marry you, Billy."

"That's a lie!" Van Buskirk's voice was hollow.

"No, it ain't. She wanted to make trouble between you and me. She's afraid of me, Billy. She wanted you to kill me."

"Oh hell! You're talking crazy."

"She set Teague on her father," Squanto said. "Fred was honest and he was trying to make her hold up her end of a bargain."

"His bargain, Squanto."

"No, it was hers."

"How would you know?"

"I know, believe me," Squanto said. "And you saw the way Teague looked at her a while ago. She set him on her father, just the same as she set us on Roby. Remember that, Billy?"

"Are you trying to scare me away from her?"

"You're not man enough to handle her. She'd ruin you."

"Goddamn you!" Van Buskirk said.

"In a way I am trying to scare you off, but it's for your own good."

"You miserable—"

"The shooting today was a little too much," Squanto said. "I can't say she rigged it, but I wouldn't be surprised if she had. Grandma Varnum is going to leave. You could see that with half an eye. Clinton is fed up. He'll leave too. Before it's over, you're going to leave because you ain't got the stomach to take her as she is."

"Of course *you* have. You're tricky, Squanto. Teague always said so. But it won't work with me."

"I think it will. She's going to find herself suddenly alone here. You know what, Billy? I think she'll do an about-face and ask you again to marry her."

"Again? I asked her."

"Did you?" Squanto smiled. "That day you two sat on the bench by the spring, who did the asking?"

207

Van Buskirk's eyes narrowed. He shot a quick look toward the bunkhouse.

"She may ask you to marry her, Billy, and then she'll do her best to see that you don't live long."

In the living room June appealed to Grandma Varnum. "That was a filthy trick of Squanto's to try to make a dying man say he had killed my father. But Teague didn't say—"

"No, he didn't say it." Grandma Varnum stared like a gray old ghost and her eyes were burning points of bitterness. "And he didn't *say* why he did it either, did he?"

"You don't believe I—"

"Talked Teague into killing your father?" The old woman nodded. She got up slowly and walked away.

"You're no angel!" June shouted. "I've guessed the truth about you. You were nothing but a common—"

The door of Grandma Varnum's room closed. June hesitated a moment and then she went outside.

Van Buskirk rose quickly. He pointed toward the bunkhouse. "I know now why Squanto thinks he knows everything that happens around here. Clinton tells him. Clinton even told him about the day I asked you to marry me."

June nodded. Cold fury came to her eyes. "I see." She started down the steps.

"He's leaving you anyway," Squanto said.

June went on as if she had not heard.

Rodney and Emma Varnum were coming down the road in a buggy.

Troy Clinton faced the heat of June's anger without showing emotion.

"So you've been a dirty spy all the time, telling Squanto lies about everything you heard around here."

"Never told him a lie," Clinton said.

"After everything I've done for you, you filthy old wreck! You drunken fool!"

Clinton made no defense.

"You're fired! Get out!"

"Sure." Clinton did not say that he was going anyway, that his warbag was already packed.

When June went outside, the Varnums were in the yard. Grandma Varnum called to them from the doorway, "Just a minute. I've got to get my trunk." Squanto went inside to help the old woman. Van Buskirk walked toward the corrals, as if going to saddle his horse.

June whirled and went back into the bunkhouse. "I've changed my mind, Troy. You can stay. There's no place for you to go, anyway."

"No, there ain't," Clinton said tonelessly.

"Just keep your mouth shut, understand?" June did not wait for an answer. She watched through the window as the Varnums drove away. The loss of Grandma Varnum hurt. She had been able to whet her ideas on the old woman's knowledge of men, and Grandma Varnum's presence had given the place an air of respectability.

Aside from that, Grandma Varnum had been a pious old fool.

Clinton went out and June did not glance around, but when she saw him crossing the yard with his warbag on his shoulder, panic struck her. He was leaving, after all. And Van Buskirk had gone to saddle his horse, and there was Squanto sitting on the porch as if he never would leave.

She had feared Teague ever since the day she wept and lied and sent him up the road in a smoking rage against her father. He was gone now, but Squanto was still here, and he was worse than Teague because she could no longer fool him. He was a patient monster trying to trap her.

Van Buskirk was the solution; he was the most easily handled. She kept herself from running as she left the bunkhouse. Van Buskirk was not saddling up. He was standing at the corral watching Clinton.

When she walked up to Van Buskirk he looked at her with such an odd hesitancy that she knew doubts were beginning to work in him.

She said, "I've been so upset I didn't know what I was doing or saying, Billy." She paused, lowering her gaze. "I still want to marry you, Billy."

Van Buskirk did not answer. When she looked up she saw that he was staring across the yard at Squanto.

"Don't believe anything he says, Billy."

But Van Buskirk was believing and the shock was on his face.

"Right away, tomorrow," June said. "We can go to town and get married."

When Van Buskirk at last looked squarely at her, he was a stranger. "It's—it's just like Squanto said." He had a feeling of horror such as he had not experienced since the day on Los Pinos. He turned away from June suddenly, ducking between the bars of the corral gate.

Squanto was watching, unmoving, stolid, still sitting on the porch.

On her way into the house June stopped to curse him. Squanto eyed her steadily. He said, "Don't use that kind of language." There was strain in his voice she had never heard before, a warning that even awesome patience could be drawn too thin.

June ran into the house.

After a time Van Buskirk rode up to the porch. His voice was uncertain. "It's been a long time since this started, ever since—" He would not say Los Pinos, and he did not want to think of Fred Darland. "You said you'd outlast us, Squanto. Now you have, but do you really—After what we know, do you really—"

"Yes," Squanto said. "I think I still want her." For a moment he looked like a man no longer sure of himself.

"Teague—the poor devil. He had that mean streak in him, Squanto, but she worked on him."

"Yeah," Squanto said.

Van Buskirk started to dismount. "I don't want him left here."

"I'll take him home after a while."

Van Buskirk hesitated. "All right." He settled into the saddle again. "I'll wait at his place." He started away slowly. At the gate he looked back. When he was on the road he went like demons were lashing him.

Clinton rode up to the porch. He waited, saying nothing, appearing reluctant to make the final move.

"How much does she owe you?" Squanto asked.

Clinton told him and Squanto went inside. The house

was deathly quiet. He supposed June was in one of the bedrooms. He rummaged in the cubbyholes of a secretary to find writing material.

Squanto was startled when June spoke suddenly from the kitchen doorway. "I'll write my own checks, Squanto."

She went outside and paid Clinton. Squanto heard her say, "You're a fool to leave here, Troy."

"I guess," Clinton said.

A strange heaviness was on Squanto as he went outside and stood with June and watched Clinton ride away. An old man with an ancient Texas rig and a faded warbag, an old man riding stiffly to nowhere. His going increased Squanto's growing indecision.

Gentle dusk was on the land. The dying coals of the barbecue pit made a faint glow. Down in the meadows the Tumbling made its low, steady sound, and from around the cooling beef came the obscene buzzing of a host of blowflies.

"What else can you think of to do?" June said bitterly. "Now that you've run everyone away from me."

"Everyone but me. I'm still here."

"I'd like to know why. You claim you know everything there is to know about me. Now I suppose you'll stand there and say that, someday, you're still going to ask me to marry you."

"I don't know," Squanto said slowly. "Yesterday I did. Now I don't honestly know."

"Yes you do," June said. "You'll be underfoot the rest of my life, if you can manage it."

Squanto was silent.

"It's another one of your little tricks," June said. "You'll be back."

"I don't know."

June peered closely into his face. She saw the truth and it scared her. "You'll be back!" she cried. She began to beat against Squanto's chest with her fists. After a time he caught both her wrists with one hand. He shook his head slowly, puzzled.

"Squanto! You're not going to leave me all alone here!"

"I'm thinking of it, June."

"No, Squanto! You can't do that! I don't know why I've done some of the things I did. I don't know, honestly. But you're not going to run away from me like the rest, are you?"

He released her hands. She crept against him, trembling, sobbing like a frightened child. This was the woman he had caught glimpses of before, a woman afraid and regretful. The wonder of beauty and frailty and evil so strangely tangled confused Squanto.

He stared at the cabin wall. He was no philosopher to explain away June's acts. He knew only that he loved her.

"Squanto, please! You won't run away like the others, will you?"

"No, I won't. I guess I love you too much for my own good, June. I can't let any other man have you. If that ever happened, I think I'd follow him around the world to kill him."

June was trembling when he took her inside. "You get some rest," he said. "I'll take Teague home. I'll send

213

someone down tomorrow to straighten up the place for you."

He drove away not long afterward, towing his horse behind the wagon. The house was dark and the glow from the barbecue pit was dimming.

And in the dark house June was sprawled across a bed, thinking. She had been desperate today when she threw herself at Van Buskirk, thinking to use him as an escape from Squanto. Then later she could have used him as she pleased; but now she knew it would not have solved her problem with Squanto.

Squanto would follow her forever, a remorseless beast seeking to crush her resistance with his terrible patience. His only weakness was his love for her, but even that was mixed with devilish ingenuity. Still, it was his love that she could use to rid herself of him.

She was finished in the Tumbling country and now she was glad that it was so. Her ambitions here, which had once seemed so great, were really petty; but at least she had learned how to deal with men and that was all she needed. In the world that Grandma Varnum talked of there were men with wealth and position, men who would not glance twice at these cow-country fools she had used to sharpen her claws.

All men were the same, no matter what they wore or how they talked. Henceforth, when she set them against each other, it would be for something greater than the savage satisfaction of making them fight like curs. She rose and lit a lamp and looked at herself critically in a mirror. She smiled at herself, knowing that she would get along all right wherever she went.

All that stood between her and the future was Squanto. Thinking out the problem, she turned away suddenly from what she saw in the mirror, but her mind went on working.

Under the cold stars a few rods short of Twelve Mile Bridge, Clinton met Charlie Nye.

"Looking for me?" the deputy asked.

"Nope."

"How's Teague?"

"Dead."

"They generally are, up this way, before I get around," Nye said. "Angus' boys said it was a fair fight."

Clinton made no comment.

"Was it?" Nye asked.

"Yeah."

"You saw it?"

"Yeah," Clinton said.

"Teague started it?"

"Uh-huh."

"Who was with Teague when he died?"

"Van Buskirk, Squanto, maybe Grandma Varnum."

"June?" the deputy asked.

"Maybe."

"So you're leaving, Troy? You'll stop awhile in town, I suppose?"

"I might."

"I'll see you there."

"Won't do you any good," Clinton said.

"Well, I'll stand the drinks anyway."

"I'll be drunk already, but that still won't do you

any good, Charlie."

"All right. I'll still buy a round."

"Help me with the chores, if you want to. We can play pitch again too. Still won't do you any good."

Clinton rode into the night.

"I don't believe it will, at that," Nye muttered. He went on toward the Tumbling.

He turned in the saddle and yelled, "You'll meet Doc Albright somewhere on the road. Tell him to turn around, will you?"

Clinton did not answer, but Nye knew the message would be delivered. He debated the worth of going all the way to Buffalo Meadows to get McQuiston's statement, and decided it would not be worth the effort, if all the other statements he picked up along the Tumbling agreed with what the Copperwhaites and Clinton had said.

CHAPTER 21

For three days after the fight no news came up to McQuiston and Calistro. Then Bill Minot, the wrinkled little rider who had accompanied June on her visit to the park the day she hauled Corbett's body out, came by to tell Calistro that June wanted him to come down and break the horses as he had promised.

Minot was towing a packhorse, going back to cow camp with supplies, and he had taken this roundabout way to deliver the message.

"Did Teague die?" McQuiston asked.

Minot nodded. "That night." He looked at Calistro. "She said to be sure and come down tomorrow morning.

Even if you don't want to break the horses, she wants to know because there's another man she can get this week if you ain't going to do it. Well, I got a long ways to ride. So long."

"So soon after—after everything down there," Calistro murmured, frowning, "she is with haste to have the horses broken?" He shrugged. "Except that I promised the old one who lives with her, I would not go."

He was leaving the next morning when McQuiston said, "See if you can find out from Grandma Varnum what June thinks about—Oh, hell, let it go."

"That is best. Such things you should find out for yourself."

McQuiston was in an unsettled mood all day. For a while he worked at repairing weak places in the fence, but he lost interest and could not hold himself to the job. Once he was on the verge of riding to the Y to talk to June, but maybe it was better to give her a little more time. He decided to wait until Calistro returned.

In late afternoon Rodney Varnum came pounding down the park on a tired horse. He dismounted and stripped the saddle and then he said quietly, "Calistro is at my place with a bullet through his chest. We've sent for the doctor, but I'm afraid it was useless."

"Who did it?"

"Squanto brought him in."

"I asked who did it!"

Rodney gave McQuiston a dark stare. "I don't know. Squanto says *he* did. He says they met in the road and had a quarrel."

McQuiston was ready to go in a few minutes.

Rodney said, "I wouldn't get too excited, McQuiston, before you know all the facts. Charlie Nye has been around the country the last few days. I sent a man to Hosmer's to get Nye before I left. You'd better let Nye handle things."

Grandma Varnum and Nye were sitting in the room with Calistro when McQuiston arrived. They watched McQuiston quietly and there was no need to inquire about Calistro's condition. A long glance told McQuiston that he was dying.

He leaned over the bed and talked softly in Spanish. There was no movement at all from Calistro. His eyes were closed and the high brown color of his face was fading.

McQuiston looked at Nye. "Where's Squanto?"

"He went home before I got here. He'll be there when we want to talk to him."

"Not 'we,' not 'talk,' Nye."

"We'll wait and see," the deputy said calmly. He nodded toward Calistro.

The room was very quiet. Somewhere in another part of the house Emma Varnum was talking to her children. Their voices rose with questions, and then there would be silences, and then Mrs. Varnum would answer. Tom Hosmer came spinning into the yard, yelling questions excitedly.

Grandma Varnum started to rise, but Emma was already outside, quieting Hosmer, keeping him from coming inside.

Some time later Rodney returned. He stood in the bedroom doorway a moment and saw everything he needed to know. He went outside to care for his horse and to answer as best he could Hosmer's questions.

Not long afterward Calistro's eyes opened and focused. McQuiston leaned over him. "How did it happen?"

Calistro looked at the strained faces around him. His lips barely moved, but the cruelty was there, the mockery, and the amused contempt for all *gringos*. "I do not know," he whispered.

"Calistro," Nye said, "who shot you?"

"I do not remember."

"Squanto?" McQuiston asked.

"I do not remember."

McQuiston asked again, pleading. Calistro's awareness was slipping fast, or perhaps he did not care to answer again, or perhaps what little was left of him was being warmed by the fierce suns of his native land and he was hearing the murmur of his own people, people who were understandable.

He died soon afterward.

Nye was waiting when McQuiston started toward his horse. "You can go along," the deputy said, "but it's mainly my business."

"Not quite." McQuiston started to swing up. "My part of the business comes first."

Nye drew his pistol. "If you start toward that gate without me, I'll have the bay with the first shot. If you want to argue after that, you'll get the second one."

The two men watched each other for several instants. Charlie Nye, small and mild-looking, was not bluffing.

"All the hanging and killing that's gone on up here has left me running in circles. Now when I'm about to get somewhere, you're not going to wreck it, McQuiston."

"If you're going with me, you'd better get a move on," McQuiston said.

"It's you that's going with me. Don't make a mistake about that."

Nye and McQuiston rode away together a few minutes later.

In the canyon, the deputy asked, "Why did he bring Calistro to the Varnum place? From where he told Rodney it happened it was a lot closer to the Y."

"Maybe he thought June Darland had enough trouble."

Nye spaced his words slowly. "Maybe he did." They went a quarter of a mile at a fast walk before the deputy spoke again. "According to Rodney, Squanto said he met Calistro coming up the road and they had a quarrel over something. Squanto didn't say what."

"I don't care what the quarrel was about. Squanto never got Calistro in a fair fight. There's no man in this country that could have."

"Maybe not," Nye said. "Where was Calistro headed this morning?"

"To the Y."

"What for?"

"To break some horses for June Darland."

"Oh, I see," Nye said mildly. "What time did he leave the park?"

"Early this morning."

"What was he doing riding *up* the Tumbling road then, around noon?"

"How would I know? Maybe he left when he found out Grandma Varnum wasn't at the Y. He said the only reason he was going there was because he'd promised her, not June, to do the work."

"I see. He didn't like Miss Darland then?"

"No, he didn't."

"Why would it take him till noon to find out Grandma Varnum wasn't at the Y?"

"That doesn't mean anything!" McQuiston said. "Squanto could have lied about the time, the place, and the reason. All I know is that he never shot Calistro in a fair fight."

"I'm sure of it," Nye said. "He didn't shoot Calistro in any kind of fight."

"He admitted it!"

"I know that, and it tangles up my job something awful. See that you don't make it worse. When we get to Squanto's place, I'll do the talking. If you try to jump him, you're going to have two men to fight."

Immediately Nye dropped a half length behind and he held the position all the way to Squanto's place. The ranchhouse sat in the open, protected only by a willow thicket behind it. On their way toward it McQuiston and Nye rode past a large log building under construction.

Squanto came from the house to meet them. He was armed. He stood there big and solid, waiting.

Nye swung down quickly. "Remember what I said, McQuiston." The deputy kept several feet away from McQuiston as they walked toward Squanto. Suddenly they had gone far enough, for the man's attitude warned them to stop.

The deputy said, "I want to know what Teague told you before he died."

"Very little," Squanto said.

"Did he mention Fred Darland?"

Squanto shook his head.

"Grandma Varnum said different."

"Talk to her then," Squanto said.

"I did. I want your evidence too. I want to know if Teague indicated who incited him to kill Darland."

"It's too late to hang Teague," Squanto said.

"You do admit then that he confessed he killed Darland?"

"It's ancient history," Squanto said. He watched McQuiston.

"Did he say who talked him into it, or did he indicate in any way——"

"Forget all that, Nye," McQuiston said. "We've got other business here."

"It'll wait," the deputy said. "You're going to wait too, McQuiston."

Charlie Nye was as competent as any man McQuiston had ever known. There was nothing to do but wait for a chance. If McQuiston could get two feet closer, he could reach the deputy. Then the rest would be with Squanto only.

"I met Troy Clinton when he was leaving," Nye said. "He told me the truth about Miss Darland and Roby."

"McQuiston knows that," Squanto said. "I told him. What are you trying to work up to, Charlie?"

"To who killed Calistro."

"I did," Squanto said.

Nye watched McQuiston. "Another thing Clinton told me was that Miss Darland spurred Teague into shooting her father."

"Clinton never told you anything, Charlie," Squanto said. "You're starting too far back and you're wasting breath trying to stop a fight between me and McQuiston."

The deputy's stride was broken. Still, he held his poise; but McQuiston, edging a few inches closer to him, saw that sweat was breaking out on Nye's face.

"You killed Calistro?" Nye asked.

"I shot him," Squanto said.

"About noon?"

"Yes."

"Uh-huh," Nye said. "About three miles from the Varnum place?"

Squanto nodded.

"Grandma Varnum saw you go by a little past nine. A mile an hour, Squanto?"

Squanto did not answer.

"You say you met him when he was riding *up* the road, Squanto? Is that right?"

Again Squanto did not answer. Respect for the deputy's sharp mind was in his look, and Squanto seemed to be seeking a way around a trap.

This was the first break in his manner. Eager to exploit it, Nye forgot McQuiston for too long a moment. "You went clear to the Y, Squanto," Nye said. "I think I know what—"

McQuiston made his step and drove a long-reaching arm at the deputy. The blow took Nye under the ear and knocked him completely off his feet. He lit in a pile of log peelings beside a carpenter's horse, unconscious when he landed.

Squanto showed no surprise as he watched McQuiston.

"Now," McQuiston said.

Squanto was wooden featured. His arms were slack at full length and he looked as slow and lumpish as McQuiston had ever seen him, as if he intended to make no fight, or did not care if he was beaten. His willingness to die gave McQuiston pause, a strange sensation of wrongness.

"Why'd you shoot him, Squanto?"

"That don't matter."

"Why'd you shoot him!"

"An argument," Squanto said.

"Was it a fair fight?"

Again Squanto considered a question as if he knew it held a trap. His hesitation rapped the wedge of doubt in McQuiston. "No," Squanto said.

Evidence that McQuiston had not believed before poured through his mind. One thought begot another because a willingness to believe had been forced on McQuiston. He said, "I don't think you would have cheated to get Ben, and I know you couldn't have got him otherwise. You didn't kill him, Squanto."

Squanto's attitude denied nothing, affirmed nothing.

"Who did it?"

A haunted expression came into Squanto's eyes. He was no longer paying attention to McQuiston; he looked like a bewildered man who could not believe his own thoughts.

"Who did it!" McQuiston knew the answer. It sickened him. "I don't believe it!"

Squanto was staring at him, but Squanto was not seeing him. *I've never been such a fool,* McQuiston thought. Saying nothing, Ben Calistro had told him that all along; dying, Calistro had continued to mock him with truth unspoken. An instinct to defend himself made McQuiston shout silently that Squanto was the biggest fool of all.

The silent block of man before McQuiston refuted the thought without trying to, and McQuiston saw more truth that followed shock too closely to be startling: Squanto was the kind of fool he had chosen to be, not a man blinded by the lies of a woman. He had walked his own path to the point of dying for her. It could not be all brutal stubbornness; the haunted expression said something different.

Squanto Whitcomb, even though he now looked like a crumbling block of granite, stood above all other men.

McQuiston's voice was curious with awe. "You'll go back to her?"

"No. I've gone as far as I can." Squanto looked then like a man who had laid down a crushing burden, but who had laid it down unwillingly. He walked away, going toward the new house under the hill.

It was then McQuiston saw that Nye was sitting up, sitting with a pistol in his hand.

McQuiston and the deputy rode away. Squanto was standing before the unfinished house and he paid no attention to their going. McQuiston looked back when they reached the road. Squanto was walking slowly along the hillside.

The big, unfinished structure, the small buildings beyond it, and the huge figure pacing the hillside suddenly made a scene that was to lie always, lonely and pathetic, in McQuiston's mind.

Far down the river Nye said, "I'll go to the Y and I won't be able to prove anything. What would you do if you were in my place?"

"I don't know."

When McQuiston returned to Buffalo Meadows, the beauty of the park was sham. He and Calistro had beaten the men who tried to keep them from this place, but that victory was nothing. A woman had taken everything from Calistro and much from McQuiston.

The fault was all McQuiston's. He went toward the cabin reluctantly. The bitterness of being a fool keened through his mind like a winter wind. Buffalo Meadows would be forever lonely, forever stained with unpleasant memories.

Tomorrow he would go to Angus Copperwhaite and tell him to come and get the cows.

Charlie Nye's frustration was threatening to engulf his patience as he prowled around the Y, with June Darland following him wherever he went. The help she seemed anxious to give him was more galling than her smile. Nye kept clenching his jaw, compounding the ache resting there from McQuiston's blow.

He maintained his mild manner but only with an effort that amused June. Every movement he had made on behalf of law in the Tumbling country had come to nothing. Here was the woman who had made all the trouble, and she was still untouchable.

"You sent for Calistro, Miss Darland?"

"Oh yes! He had promised to break some horses. I understand he was a very good man with horses."

"And you'd arranged for Squanto to be here later the same morning?"

"Later? I don't understand, Mr. Nye. I did send Minot to tell Squanto I wanted to see him, yes."

She told the truth where truth was established; she lied where facts were hard to prove. The hellish simplicity of it outraged Nye. He asked gently, "Then Calistro never showed up here at all?"

"I didn't see him. I was in my room sewing."

That left her leeway to cover the fact that Nye had found the tracks of Calistro's pony within fifty yards of the gate. All evidence inside the gate was gone, and you couldn't take tracks into court anyway.

"Calistro came here and you shot him deliberately," the deputy said. "You figured Squanto would take everything off your hands, and he did. What did you tell him—that Calistro tried to attack you?"

"You're insulting and you're crazy!" June said.

Only two men had ever shown June Darland their complete loathing of her, Calistro, and now, Nye. The deputy shook his head slowly, pouring into his expression his opinion of her foulness. June sent back her own contempt of him, and of all men. Nye could not bear it.

"I know whores a hundred times better than you," he said. "They're human beings. You ain't."

Anger was what she wanted from him. Nye knew it. He got himself under control and tried a bluff. "I found out from Troy Clinton the other night—"

"I doubt that," June said. "But anything that comes from Clinton will be the talk of a drunken old man, a man I fired because he was useless and dishonest."

"You feel pretty safe, don't you?"

"I don't know what you mean."

"You knew Squanto would shoulder the blame for killing Calistro. You were sure McQuiston would kill him. I think you're just a little afraid of Squanto." Nye saw he was on the right track, and although it would do him no good, he would at least speak his mind.

"If you're through snooping," June said, "get out."

"You *should be* afraid of Squanto," Nye said. "Any man who will go as far as he has for you knows what he's after. I think that somewhere deep inside of you you're afraid of all men." The deputy nodded. "But you're going to have one the rest of your life— Squanto."

The white fear on June's face rose higher. "Get out!"

"I'm never going to forget what happened to Roby, to your father, and most of all—to Ben Calistro. Squanto will have to remember that too. Live with it night and day, Miss Darland. I'll always be waiting for a slip, a mistake." Nye stared at the woman for several moments. "Someday I hope to see you hanged."

The deputy walked to his horse and rode away.

CHAPTER 22

Angus Copperwhaite saw the furious dust of the buggy on the Tumbling road and wondered why the driver was in such a hurry. He recognized June Darland after she turned and was half way up his lane. He was waiting for her when the buggy spun into the yard.

"What's the trouble, June?"

"There's none. I like to drive fast, that's all." June smiled. "Mr. Copperwhaite, I want to sell everything I own—today."

The strong scent of a bargain caught Angus' interest instantly. "Well, now, that's a big order all at once, considering the way money is, and one thing and another."

"You've got the money, Mr. Copperwhaite. It's either you or two men in Columbine who made me an offer a few weeks ago. I know so little of business but I do know that I can trust you, so I came here first."

"That's the sad part of it," Angus said, "you can trust me, but I make a hard bargain." He looked at a small trunk in the back of the buggy.

Mrs. Copperwhaite came out on the porch. "Won't you come inside, June?" Her manner was civil and that was all.

"Thank you." June was on the ground before Angus could move to give her his hand.

The pleasure of bargaining would have held Angus a long time but June set a figure so quickly and held to it so strongly that Angus knew it was futile to try to get around her. He drew up a deed and wrote a check. He helped June into her buggy and watched her whirl out of the yard.

When he went inside, his wife and Evaleth stopped their conversation abruptly. "The poor lass," Angus said. "She was like a driven thing. Maybe we—"

"The poor lass got five hundred more than you once said you'd give her," Mrs. Copperwhaite said.

"And five hundred less than I would have given," Angus replied absently. "She's a pretty little thing, like a child. I find it hard to believe—" He frowned at his wife and daughter. Evaleth was staring oddly at the cat sleeping under the stove. "You women are always too hard, too quick about your opinions of other women."

Angus went out. He saw June stop her buggy for a few moments on the Tumbling road. A half hour later he saw McQuiston coming up the lane and was well pleased.

But McQuiston's reason for coming was not so good. Angus listened and spoke slowly. "I can take the herd back, of course, and at no loss to you, since the cows have had the benefit of that fine grass, but—Let's go down to my medicine chest."

They had a drink. McQuiston's mood was dark.

"It's because of Calistro?" Angus asked.

"Partly."

"And Squanto—did you—"

"No. He and I will have no trouble."

"That's good," Angus said. "Although I don't understand it." He left no prying silence. "I see no need for you to run away. I'll give you a business proposition, McQuiston, land here on the river and terms you can meet."

"What land?"

Angus hesitated. "The Y. I've just bought it."

McQuiston stared at him. "She's gone?"

"About an hour ago. You'll have a good start there, and you can find a way to hold on to the meadows too. It's being done all the time."

"Who was with her?"

"She was alone," Angus said. "I gathered she was leaving the country. Stay here a day or two, McQuiston, and we'll talk over the deal."

"All right."

Later, in the house, Evaleth said, "We were sorry to hear about Ben Calistro." She made her statement and turned away. McQuiston watched her going toward the kitchen.

The hospitality of the Copperwhaites that asked nothing in return, the warmth and feeling of their family spirit began to thaw some of the loneliness in McQuiston as he sat and talked with Angus of the possibilities at the Y.

CHAPTER 23

Urgency was driving June Darland as she left the Copperwhaite place. Charlie Nye's insight, which she considered devilish and cruel, had heightened her fear of Squanto. She was convinced now that Squanto had accepted the blame for killing Calistro not because of love for her, but because his evil, cunning mind had seen a way to get a hold on her.

But it was not too late to escape him. Once she was

fairly away from him, let him try to find her. His talk about following her around the world had scared her too much. The world was big; all she needed was a head start.

She kept looking up the valley as she raced down the lane. She saw something and fear caught in her throat, but between the dust and the jolting she was not certain that what she had seen was a rider. When she reached the road she stopped.

It was a rider. He was far up the valley, too far to tell about his speed or the color of his horse, and for a time, even his direction of travel. Her heart was thumping as she forced herself to peer across the green distance and gauge the man's movement by landmarks.

Yes, he was coming toward her and he seemed to be moving fast. Squanto!

Terror flayed her then. She sent the horse ahead with a lunge that popped the traces. She went around the shoulder of a hill and the valley was cut from view. The terror pressed more heavily then.

Squanto, remorseless, slow, coming to cut her off from a new life, to hold her forever with fear.

Down the long sage hills she fled, whipping the dust behind her. Her trunk was awash against the side-boards from the lurching of the buggy. She fled from Squanto Whitcomb. A strong and competent driver, she took the curves without slacking, guiding the horse where she wanted it to go, steadying it in its run but not sparing it.

Light wood and metal groaned as she sent the buggy up and down the dips, as she bounced through gully crossings where sand stilled the grinding of the wheels for a few moments before the horse lunged up to the lava rock again.

The horse was strong. It ran with a reaching stride, with foam spinning from its muzzle. She weighed the animal's strength against the distance to the river and was willing to kill the horse to get there quickly. At Twelve Mile ranch she could get another horse, and kill it too if need be to make the eastbound train in Columbine.

On the long, gentle run above Claussen Breaks she twisted to look back. The wind was laying the dust of her flight to the west and she could see through the thin haze not yet settled to the top of the hills near the Tumbling.

No one was in sight. She had gained on Squanto. But the thought was part wish and it turned uneasy at once. He had cut through the hills, angling to reach the road to Broken Forge. He would ride like he did everything else, with calculated lack of haste, and he would still be able to cut her off somewhere on the road to Columbine. He would be there waiting, a monster of patience; and because he knew the truth about Calistro, she would have to do as he commanded. He would smile and say, *I've been waiting.*

Her flight became a pitiful struggle then. She could not turn back. She began to sob because of the injustice, the oppression that was trying to cut her off.

She reached the top of Claussen Breaks where the road snaked down over layered rocks. At the foot of the breaks lay the last easy run to Twelve Mile ranch. She could see the ranch clearly, green alfalfa fields running on the north side of the Columbine River, the restful bloom of great cottonwoods around the buildings, and a short span of railroad tracks shining in the sun this side of the cottonwoods.

All at once her problem was beaten. The answer was so simple that she laughed aloud at her panic. The west-bound train would pass in an hour. It stopped whenever it was flagged down at Twelve Mile Siding.

Let Squanto take his shortcut across the hills and wait on the Columbine road, and wait until he rotted. She took the first turn going down the breaks, over long scales of rock that pitched to the outside of the grade.

She lay back on the lines then, but the horse had the grade with it and the horse was still living its frantic run. It tried to respond to the lines, grinding its shoes. The buggy swayed, yawing toward the outside.

Unafraid, her hands strong and sure, June gained enough control to make the turn safely. The next curve was almost a continuation of the first, and sharper. The inside wheels hit a step in the rocky bed that was higher than the rest of the surface. The buggy bounced to the edge of the road, staggering the horse. A hind wheel went over.

It rode for a few moments on loose rock and almost came back on the road. Then it struck a massive thrust of ledge rock. The long spokes collapsed, tearing from the hub, splintering the rim, and the axle came down with a crash that threw the horse to its knees.

With both hands gripping the lines June shot from the seat like a rag doll hurled into the air, up and over the sage clinging to the steep hillside, up and over the great chunks of rock that had been torn from the hill to make the road. For a tick of time she was a beautiful woman sprawled in the air, with an expression of surprise, rather than fear.

The weight of the horse tore the lines from her hands and twisted her so that she fell on her back to the rocks thirty feet below. The horse lurched up, wild-eyed, heaving, standing with bleeding legs. Down in the rocks there was silence.

Tortured by the awful sickness of a week-long drunk, Troy Clinton crossed the Columbine at Twelve Mile Bridge. The booming sound of his horse on the planks added to the hollowness he felt and the rushing water seen through the cracks of the decking made him giddy. He licked his lips and spat. He was glad to reach the solidity of the far bank.

He was going back to the Y.

It was not lack of pride. He did not know what it was, unless it was the thought that he could still feel that he was useful there. June would take him back. She was alone; she needed him.

At the foot of Claussen Breaks he overtook Wilson and Koering in a light spring wagon. Knowing his taciturnity, the engineers greeted him and made no attempt to strike up a running conversation. Clinton rode along beside them. After a time, observing his sad condition, Wilson made the mistake of asking Clinton if he wanted to ride for a while in the wagon.

"Hell no! What do I look like?"

"I just thought—" Wilson let it go.

Part way up the hill they found the horse with the smashed buggy. Koering said, "That looks like June Darland's—by God, it is!"

Clinton was looking ahead to marks that showed the horse had dragged the wrecked buggy from somewhere farther up the hill. "Cut it loose!" he cried, and spurred his horse into a plunging run, holding over so he could see below the road.

He was carrying June Darland up from the dry wash when Wilson and Koering saw him again. Wilson went sliding down the hill to help him. Clinton said, "Get out of the way." His face was gray and terrible.

After he reached the road he was trembling and gasping so that he could hardly speak, still holding June in his arms.

"Is she—" Wilson looked at Koering, and both knew there was no need to finish the question.

"Clear that junk out of the wagon," Clinton said.

They were slow and careful with the cases that held Brunton compasses and their transit. "Throw it out of there!" Clinton said. He saw everything they did and yet the engineers felt that he did not know they were present.

They crowded their gear in front and went up the road, towing the limping buggy horse and Clinton's mount. Clinton sat in back, holding June. They started to go on past the lane to the Copperwhaite place and Clinton said, "Turn here, damn you!"

He still held June after they reached the buildings. No man could talk to him. He admitted that June was dead

236

and gave her up only when Mrs. Copperwhaite took charge. After that Clinton seemed to be himself, flaring up savagely only once when Angus said something about taking June on to the Y.

"No! That place was no good for her!"

McQuiston and Dan Copperwhaite rode all that night and part of the next day to find Squanto, who had been out on his range since the day McQuiston and Nye had talked to him. He came back with them and they waited outside his house while he changed clothes.

McQuiston kept staring at the big, unfinished log house under the hill.

Once more people came from all around the Tumbling country to see June Darland, malice and curiosity and charity commingling.

McQuiston was unweeping, with all the sad compassion of an Irish spirit in his face. Billy Van Buskirk cried like a child bereft. A small smile was on June's face. She looked fragile, unbroken, beautiful. McQuiston tried to cling to the story she had told him of running with her face uplifted to the rising sun.

Grandma Varnum wept silently, her harsh old face looking toward the western mountains, toward some kind of understanding which she could not find here.

Squanto Whitcomb was unbowed, standing with his legs like great posts rooted into the earth. Something was smashed in him but he was too strong to be broken. When he started away, McQuiston sought to speak to him, but Squanto did not notice. He got on his horse and rode away, a tremendous figure who soon grew small and lonely against the greenness of the valley.

The general drifting away began. Angus came over to McQuiston. "I've work here for Clinton, if he wants it." Angus frowned thoughtfully. "That is, if you haven't figured to let him homestead Buffalo Meadows for you."

"You've asked him that already, haven't you?"

"It happened that I did," Angus said. "It's lonely up there, but that's what he said he wanted."

McQuiston saw Evaleth going toward the house. He said, "I'll talk to Clinton."

Evaleth looked back over her shoulder at him, promising nothing, giving no invitation. The grave on the hill was behind McQuiston. He kept his back to it and thought of the long years ahead and he was sure of what he could do with them.

He watched Evaleth go into the house. Angus walked away with a quiet smile.

Center Point Publishing

600 Brooks Road • PO Box 1
Thorndike ME 04986-0001 USA

(207) 568-3717

US & Canada:
1 800 929-9108